Live To Kill
A Steve Dane Thriller

Brian Drake

WOLFPACK
PUBLISHING
— EST 2013 —

The characters and events portrayed in this book are
fictitious. Any similarity to real persons, living or dead,
is coincidental and not intended by the author.

Text copyright © 2021 (As Revised) Brian Drake

Published by Wolfpack Publishing
5130 S. Fort Apache Road, 215-380
Las Vegas, NV 89148

Paperback IBSN 978-1-64734-739-0
eBook ISBN 978-1-64734-738-3

Live To Kill

Chapter One

Two men in their early 60s stepped off the jetliner into the terminal at San Remo International Airport. The air-conditioned terminal would only provide a short respite from the heat and humidity they faced once they stepped outside.

"Is it going to be miserable our entire stay?" said Perry Royce as he walked with the help of a cane in his right hand. When they moved from carpet onto tile and followed arrows to baggage claim, the tip of the can made a dull thud on the floor as he moved.

George DeRocca, to Royce's right, smiled. "It's like coming home."

Both Royce and DeRocca were veteran officers with the Central Intelligence Agency. While Royce's specialty had been the Middle East, and he spoke expert Farsi and Arabic, he had never once set foot in Central America. That meant his Spanish was nonexistent.

DeRocca, on the other hand, had spent many years in various postings between Colombia, Honduras, and elsewhere south of the border. He spoke flawless Spanish and promised to help guide them out of the airport. They had a ride waiting for them, and appropriate accommodations, so there would be no reason to deal with taxi drivers or hotel staff.

Both men had been classmates at Harvard, political science majors, when they caught the attention of CIA recruiters. It helped Royce's case that his father had once been DCI before an accidental drowning during a fishing trip cut short his career and legacy. The old man's shoes had been hard to fill, with colleagues always comparing Royce the Younger to his old man, but Perry felt he'd done his father proud, serving with distinction, retiring with full benefits, as well the profits from a side business that guaranteed him a safety net for the rest of his life.

Killing a few people to acquire that safety net was all in the details.

Royce had brought DeRocca and one other man into their scheme, and the absence of the third man weighed on them both as they collected their bags and emerged from the terminal into the heat and wet. Royce felt moisture on his skin straight away.

Daniel Gallagher, the third man, hadn't been able to make the trip because he was dying of cancer.

Gallagher he was one of the reasons they were visiting San Remo. They needed to speak with other associates about what to do with poor Daniel. They had other topics on the agenda, but Royce figured Gallagher would take up the most time.

A blacked-out GMC Yukon waited for the pair, and they climbed into the air-conditioned vehicle and began a long drive into the mountains. Royce sighed with relief at the blast of cool air. DeRocca seemed unbothered either way.

San Remo had its share of urban development, but outside the cities near the coast, forest dominated the landscape. Lush green as far as the eye could see. Royce stared out the window without truly comprehending the view.

His thoughts were with his dying compatriot. Compatriot was too soft a word. They were friends from years back. Gallagher had not attended Harvard like Royce and DeRocca but came from an equally prosperous background. The CIA had discovered Gallagher at Yale.

For a long time at CIA headquarters, the Gang of Three, as they'd been called, ran the show with the DCI above them. They were all retired now, devoted to the "other thing" that they'd started, and Royce now considered them a corner of a triangle topped by the man they were traveling to see. Another party, a crime syndicate in Washington, DC, occupied the third corner of the triangle. Royce did not like being subservient to another. The original scheme had been his idea, and for a long time, he was top dog. Royce was not unrealistic, however. If he was going to meet his goals and desires, compromises had to be made, and it didn't hurt that the top man had an immense amount of power and money to wield.

Royce was glad for the comfort for the vehicle because it was a slow ride out of the city. San Remo, while firmly controlled by President-for-Life Diego Marco, had a big problem. Rebels out to depose Marco had nearly managed to plunge the nation into full-blown civil war. So far, Marco's forces had limited their attacks and kept them on the run in the forests, but the military presence, needed for security, was everywhere.

Tanks at intersections. Armed soldiers on patrol. Civilians avoiding the soldiers' gazes, now and then troops dragging somebody out of a building, somebody who tried to fight back and was thus clubbed over the head. Obvious undesirables. Rebel sympathizers. Royce had seen similar situations all around the world, but this one was a bit more personal. If President Diego Marco didn't clear out the rebel forces, the Big Scheme might fall apart entirely.

Up a winding mountain road, the GMC engine purred quietly. Presently they drove through a gate manned by armed troopers, all wearing the uniform of the San Remo army.

"Lassen gets around," Royce said.

"He wasn't kidding."

Other troops not in uniform dotted the expansive estate, with its high wall and ornate architecture. The GMC stopped at the front steps, where a tall man with blue eyes and a sharply creased white suit waited for them. His smile showed perfect teeth.

Perry Royce had not liked Cyrus Lassen at first but grew to admire the man who operated in the shadows of the underworld. It had been Lassen's idea for Royce and his crew to branch out south of the border, create a safe haven for their criminal enterprises with the protection of the San Remo government, where there was no extradition treaty with the United States or any other western government.

"Welcome, my friends," Lassen said. He shook the hands of both men as attendants lifted their luggage out of the GMC. Behind Lassen stood a burly man whom Lassen introduced as Sanchez, the man in charge of the security force on the estate. Royce examined the man. Puffy black hair, dark skin, a mole on his chin.

Lassen's wrist sparkled with a Rolex Sea Dweller; the diamond ring on his left hand also stated his status. He was the money man. The visionary. The man who had his fingers in a thousand different pies around the world, and yet remained off the radar of police, Interpol, and Western intelligence.

Royce and DeRocca had only learned of Lassen's existence when he chose to reveal himself and extend an invitation to visit the estate and make an offer the two men couldn't refuse. Years ago. Almost a decade. And while Royce knew he was getting older, Lassen appeared not to have aged a day.

"We'll get you to your rooms so you can settle down," Lassen said. "Dinner at 8, and then we will talk on the deck and enjoy a beautiful evening. We have much to discuss. Follow me!"

Lassen and his visitors, trailed by the burly Sanchez, entered the house.

Royce kept his face stoic. He had to hide the pit in his stomach. He knew the conversation regarding Gallagher would take a grim turn.

He had to mentally prepare to agree to execute his friend.

Chapter Two

Lassen's kitchen staff prepared a five-course meal and it was marvelous and almost made Royce forget why they were there. The men did not discuss business during dinner, but instead caught up on trivial matters. Sports. Music. Even a trio of men contemplating the takeover of a small nation in Central America liked to talk about fun things.

Lassen and DeRocca had a particular fondness for soccer, although DeRocca had to refer to it as "football" since they were south of the border.

On the back deck as evening took hold, the brilliant orange sunlight over the tops of trees a truly dazzling sight, Lassen's servants brought drinks. Lassen, Royce, and DeRocca sat on a crescent-shaped wicker couch, facing each other, with a table in the center.

They had dressed casually for dinner at Lassen's insistence, and Royce was glad. His slacks and polo made the hot night bearable.

"I hope you enjoyed the dinner," Lassen said. "I wanted to avoid unpleasant talk under we finished."

"I thought so," Royce said.

DeRocca only nodded.

Lassen crossed his legs. "We have some problems."

"The first of which," DeRocca started, "is the situation with the rebels. We saw nothing but tanks and soldiers on the ride in."

"The tanks blocked the view of the McDonalds," Royce said.

Lassen glanced at Royce without as much as a smirk. He said, "I talk daily with President Marco. He assures me the rebels are subdued and on the run. In fact, lately, they've taken an interest in me occupying this place. It's the presidential retreat in San Remo, did you know that?"

"We did not," Royce said.

"That's how well Marco and I get along. I get the vacation home. Anyway, now and then rebels drift in my direction, and I like to grab one or two and let them go without any weapons."

"What purpose does that serve?" Royce said.

"My man Sanchez and his team chase them. If the rebels are able to get away, they earn their freedom and can return to the war. Most don't make it. My troops are very good man-trackers." Now Lassen smiled. "It's entertaining."

"No syndicate or independent organization will want the sanctuary we offer in San Remo," DeRocca said, "if there's a civil war going on. Why are we bothering to send weapons and equipment from the US if they aren't being used?"

"They are being used, George. You saw the tanks and soldiers; you did not see fighting. The rebels are on the run. There will be no war. The majority of San Remo likes President Marco." Lassen took a deep breath. "That's enough about the rebels. We have to discuss your absent friend."

Royce and DeRocca said nothing. Royce's bourbon and water suddenly didn't agree with his stomach. He set the glass on the table.

"He has to die," Lassen said. "We cannot risk him talking before the cancer kills him."

Royce and DeRocca only stared.

Lassen regarded the two men thoughtfully. "You disagree with this?"

Royce didn't hesitate. "Greatly."

"But he is a liability."

"He's our friend."

A low chuckle bubbled from Lassen's gut. "There is no room for friends in conquest, gentleman."

"We wouldn't be here without him," DeRocca said.

"We started this together," Royce continued. "We will end it with him too."

"He'll be dead before we finish," Lassen said.

"Doesn't matter. We owe it to Daniel to stay the course and acknowledge his work."

Lassen's smile wasn't friendly. Royce didn't back down or feel intimidated. As a young CIA man, he'd faced the hardest jihadists the Middle East had to offer. Lassen had a long way to go before he reached that level of menace.

"I admire your dedication, gentlemen," Lassen continued. "But look at what we've accomplished so far. Your conspiracy put you both in positions of power deep within American intelligence. You used Operation Eagle to your advantage and eliminated—how many people?"

Royce said, "Nobody that didn't deserve it."

"Your list includes American citizens," Lassen said. "When word of that leaks out, your American press won't look favorably upon you, no matter who was killed, especially when they put the pieces together and realize the strategic importance of those killings. They brought you more power."

Royce and DeRocca said nothing. Their hard looks didn't dissuade Cyrus Lassen one inch.

Royce had always considered himself a stable man, not one prone to emotional outbursts or panicked thinking. But he was experiencing both now. He wanted to close the short distance between himself and Lassen and kill the blue-eyed dapper man in the white suit. He'd steal his Rolex and ring as souvenirs. If he had any hope of surviving the armed troopers after the fact, he might have done it. A glance at DeRocca assured Royce he'd back his play.

But Royce wasn't young anymore and his bum leg accentuated the point.

"I'm sorry," Lassen said, with no trace of actual remorse. He sounded like he was turning down a child's request for a cookie before dinner. "Daniel Gallagher is a liability. He will talk. He must be dealt with before he ruins everything we've worked for."

"No," Royce said.

Lassen's raised his voice. "You do not have an option, Perry. We are on the verge of creating a haven here in San Remo for criminals of all sorts, people who will pay us big money for sanctuary. You will both be wealthy beyond your wildest dreams. This is what we set out to do. This is what we've worked for. You want to jeopardize it now for something as trivial as friendship?"

Royce finally looked away from Lassen and let out a breath. DeRocca's shoulders sagged in surrender.

"It will be quick," Lassen said. "He's going to die anyway. Look at it as a mercy killing. If you let the cancer take him, he will be in agony for weeks or months."

Royce raised his head to meet Lassen's eyes once more, but the tall man was taking a long drink. He seemed quite satisfied with himself.

Royce could only imagine what he'd look like with his throat cut.

Chapter Three

Fear.

That's what Steve Dane saw in Nina's eyes as they faced each other across the table. She swallowed more of her screwdriver, poured immediately after the departure of Number One, after the older man had provided Dane with the name of a man who possessed information about his father's death.

"Do you want to talk about it?" Dane said.

Nina set down the glass.

"No."

"Number One can sure drop a bomb, can't he?"

"It would have been nice if you told him to get lost."

Dane fingered the piece of paper in his hand, the one he wanted, on the one hand, to burn and forget; on the other, he wanted to leave everything in the hotel room as it was and confront the man right away.

"I need to know what happened to my father."

Nina pressed her lips together. Dane raised an eyebrow.

"Don't hide from me, Nina," he said. "Communication is the key to any relationship."

"And right now, I'm communicating that I don't want to talk. Understand?"

"No, I don't."

"Stop bothering me," she said. "Call McConn and find out where this man you want so desperately to find is hiding."

"Nina."

She looked at the carpet with a clenched jaw and tight lips.

"What happened in Moscow?"

She shut her eyes and did not answer him. He waited, quietly, but then rose from the chair and took out his cell phone. He knew she could keep secrets; whatever was trapped in her head wasn't coming out without a prybar. It had to be a whopper indeed. Maybe it explained her personality.

Maybe it also explained her recurring nightmares.

He dialed Todd McConn, who had a room elsewhere in the hotel. McConn answered on the third ring.

"Already?"

"Just some background this time, Todd," Dane said, turning his back to Nina. "Daniel Gallagher." He spelled the last name. "He's either still with the CIA or retired, I'm not sure."

"Okay, hang on."

The line went quiet as McConn researched the inquiry. Dane did not turn to look at Nina. If she wanted to pout about whatever mind bomb Number One had triggered, let her. He wasn't going to beg. If she didn't want to talk, he understood, but he couldn't help but feel she wasn't talking because she didn't trust him. After all they'd been through together? It didn't make sense why she'd clam up. All the woman did every other moment of the day was run her mouth.

He understood pain at the molecular level. Was that what they were dealing with? Was he being harsh?

He finally turned when he heard liquid being poured. Nina refilled her glass. No orange juice this time. Straight vodka.

Of course. Why talk like a normal person when you can pickle your liver instead? A dark cloud settled over Dane. Was she going to be the next mess to clean up?

"You there, Steve?"

"Standing by," he said, trying not to grip the phone too tightly. Irritation overcame him. He wanted to tell her to quit acting like a five-year-old.

"Gallagher's retired and living in Virginia. Got something to write on?"

Dane moved to the nightstand, where he grabbed a cheap pen and a piece of the hotel stationery. "Go."

McConn provided the address. "You gonna need me?" he said.

"Not sure yet." Dane finished writing. "I'll let you know."

"What's the deal with this guy?"

"He knows the truth about my father."

"Are you serious?"

"The time for joking is over, Todd. Thanks for your help."

Dane cut off McConn in the middle of his good-bye.

Nina swallowed a mouthful of vodka and cursed at Dane's back.

Some things simply couldn't be spoken out loud, but she didn't know how to explain that. She was Russian. They didn't explain things. They didn't do feelings. They shut up and drank vodka.

"We know what happened in Moscow, Ms. Talikova. You might say the two of you are on a collision course with what made you."

Number One. The smug bastard. Fat son of a bitch. She could have shot him for saying that. Her past was nobody's business but hers. She swallowed another mouthful of vodka. The elixir wasn't helping. She had to admit the booze never helped at all, really.

Dane knelt at the nightstand to note the address McConn had provided. She didn't know what he saw in her eyes, but she was well aware of what she saw in his. Hope. Number One had done more than offer a name; he'd offered the young boy still within Dane's adult body the hope he needed that his father hadn't betrayed his country.

She looked into her glass. The clear vodka shimmered in the overhead light.

She never wanted to see Moscow again. The only thing waiting for her there was death.

But if they were indeed on the collision course described by Number One, she'd have to eventually face her own demons the way Dane was so bravely—or eagerly?—facing his own. He'd dive into the fire with his usual attitude while she sat drinking to make the world go away.

And that was no way to live.

Dane ended his call and finally turned to look at her. She offered half a smile.

"When do we leave?" she said.

It seemed to Dane like they were always packing and unpacking suitcases. He wondered what it might be like to have his clothes in a closet for a change. As he zipped his suitcase closed, Nina packed the last of her items and zipped her bags.

"I don't feel like flying," he told her.

"Okay."

"I've done enough flying for a while."

"Fine."

"I'll get us a car." He started for the door.

"You're only delaying the inevitable," she said.

"Look who's talking."

"Hey!"

He didn't look back. The door shut behind him.

Dane slammed the trunk lid. Déjà vu gripped him.

Every family vacation, when he was a boy, had been a road trip. A long road trip complete with chorus after chorus of "Are we there yet?" from Dane and his brother.

And here he was loading a car for another such trip, a drive where fun was not the destination, but instead destiny. A violent destiny. His goal was to clear his father's name. Somebody was going to pay for what the Dane family had suffered. If his father was indeed guilty, and Dane's hopes dashed, then he'd find a way to face that reality. But he knew his father. The man could not have been a traitor. No way. Not for anything.

His father had always said they took road trips because they were fun, but Dane wondered whether they couldn't afford to fly places or if the old man, in his constant on-and-off-an-airplane routine in his work with the US Army, was so sick of airplanes that the last thing he wanted to do was board one for a vacation. He figured the latter. He and his brother had never lacked for necessities.

Was there a reason he was reflecting on the old days? Some sort of spiritual connection with his father that he wasn't aware of? They were questions Dane didn't want to think about, but questions he also shouldn't deny.

Nina was already in the passenger seat. She hadn't

said a word since he'd left the hotel room to arrange the rental. To hell with her. He wasn't delaying anything. He wanted time to think. He didn't want to deal with a crowded airplane and its associated issues. Nina had no leg to stand on. She could sit and stew for the whole drive as far as he was concerned.

He knew her too well. She wasn't going anywhere without him.

Chapter Four

They drove in shifts, which gave them both time to nap, since neither said much. Dane kept to the coastal highway as much as possible to get a glimpse of the ocean. He didn't mind seeing the water, but also didn't want to end up submerged in it anytime soon. Their most recent adventure had provided enough swimming for a while.

Two uncomfortable days and a total of ten hours later, Dane pulled into a motel in Wilmington, North Carolina. The Motel Wilmington on South 17th Street was a basic building, nothing fancy, but looked comfortable. Bright lights lit the building on all sides. Dane checked his watch. Almost 11 p.m. He hoped it wasn't too late to get a room.

Nina finally broke the silence that had stayed with them most of the ride.

"We're not staying here," she said.

Dane popped the trunk. "Just overnight."

"They won't have room service."

"We won't be here that long, Nina."

"This is beneath us."

"They do probably offer a continental breakfast in the

morning, so it's almost the same thing," Dane said.

"A Svenhard's roll and bad coffee are hardly my idea of breakfast."

"Hey, it won't be that bad. They probably have a Keurig."

Dane left the car with Nina still stewing inside. He pulled their luggage out of the trunk, leaving the trunk open as he walked past the car and into the motel office. He didn't look back but figured Nina wasn't smiling at him. He'd left her bags behind.

The large room contained one king bed, a large-screen TV, a coffeemaker (indeed a Keurig, which made Dane laugh and Nina frown), and the usual amenities provided by such motels. Street noises were well muffled, which pleased Dane. Right now, all he wanted was quiet.

But Nina was knocking around in the bathroom creating a racket. She exited in a huff.

"The towels don't feel right."

"Nina."

"Also, we're out of booze."

"You drank it already?"

"The vodka was the last bottle we had."

Dane looked out the window at the night sky. It might be nice to get away from her for a few minutes.

"What do you want?" he said.

"Any bottle that says alcohol on it."

"You mean denatured alcohol is okay?"

"That'll kill me."

"So will the distilled stuff at the rate you're going."

"Are you leaving or not?"

Dane departed to the mumbled soundtrack of Nina cursing in her native language.

He left the building and started for the rental car, then decided to walk. The exercise would be nice after sitting for so long, but his leg muscles behind and above his knees began to cramp. He needed to stop and stretch but the hell with it. He was mad and needed to walk it off.

He looked up the area on his phone and found a liquor store two blocks away.

One of them had to extend the peace offering soon. He was forgetting what they were arguing about, and that didn't bode well. A state of conflict with Nina wasn't something Dane wished on his worst enemy. He decided to accept the fact that she wasn't going to talk about Moscow no matter how many times he asked, and she might never talk about Moscow. When she was ready to explain, she'd begin the conversation.

Dane knew very well that there were some topics that couldn't be brought up. He had his share of war stories he never wanted to relive. But to him, his relationship with Nina meant sharing the hard stuff. She'd never asked about the ghosts of battles past that Dane carried with him. Maybe she knew he wouldn't want to talk about them.

Or maybe their relationship simply existed beneath a very shallow surface.

Dane didn't like that idea at all.

He immediately dismissed the thought from his mind. Their relationship went much deeper. They'd been through too much together, and she, more than he wanted to admit, was basically his conscience. How many times had her counsel helped him figure out the solutions to the problems they faced?

She needed time. He had to allow her that time.

The chilly night air felt good on his skin, and Dane kicked himself for a major lack of situational awareness.

He was walking without checking for threats behind, in front, or on either side. Scattered vehicular traffic on the street appeared normal; no boogeymen sneaking up behind. Dane shook his head. They needed a break. He had a home in Austria and couldn't remember the color of the carpet. It might be time to head home for a while, after they finished their business in Virginia.

If there was an after.

Presently Dane stepped off the sidewalk and into the nearly empty parking lot of an Ernie's Liquor, the ubiquitous liquor store chain. Whoever Ernie was, Dane thought as he pulled open the door, he knew how to run a business. Maybe Dane and Nina could retire and open their own liquor store. He nixed the idea when he realized Nina would drink the stock and they'd quickly go bankrupt.

A flower shop would be safer.

Either way, they could set up the back room as an apartment and shoot anybody who tried to break in and steal stuff. Dane would hate to see domestication affect their body count. although he wasn't sure there was a market for stolen flowers.

The clerk behind the counter didn't take his eyes from a small television as Dane strolled up and down the spirits aisle, bottles large and small crammed close together on narrow shelves. He grabbed a bottle of Russian Standard vodka, paid without getting any eye contact from the clerk and gripped the paper bag tightly as he exited the store.

He started walking and this time focused on enjoying the exercise rather than letting his mind wander. It certainly was a nice night for a walk.

Until a woman screamed.

Dane turned around sharply. A woman, running toward

him, crossed the street against the light and almost stumbled as she gained the sidewalk. There was no mistaking the fear in her wide eyes as she continued straight for Dane, and he stepped aside lest she crash into him.

And then he saw the man chasing her. A man with a stainless-steel pistol in one hand.

Chapter Five

Dane had no gun of his own, but he did have a rather stout bottle of vodka.

He pulled the bottle out of the brown paper bag, holding it by the neck. The woman didn't continue by when she reached him. She stopped short, grabbing the front of his shirt, and let out a rush of unintelligible syllables, but the gist was that she needed help and needed it bad.

The man with the gun did not look like a cop. He was too heavy, with a thick beard. The possibility did exist, however, that he was undercover, that the woman who felt quite frail as Dane moved her aside was a suspect in a crime. But the man was not shouting, "Stop, police," or any of the usual law enforcement commands.

All bets were off.

The woman landed in the bushes off to the left and kicked up a ruckus crawling to the pavement on the other side, but Dane didn't see where she went. He closed in on the gunman, lifting the bottle high. The man stopped and tried to bring up his pistol, but Dane's swing caught him on the side of the head. The bottle hit hard, the shock of the impact against the man's hard skull sending a sting-ing sensation up Dane's right arm, but the man dropped like a puppet with cut strings, collapsing in a heap on the sidewalk.

The bottle didn't break. Dane raised an eyebrow in admiration. Only a smear of blood indicated that the bottle had been used for purposes not intended by the manufacturer.

He knelt quickly and checked the man's pockets, along his belt. No badge. Wallet full of cash and an ID. Dane tossed it aside. He stood, collecting the bottle again, and looked for the woman. She was on hands and knees be-hind the bushes, and when Dane reached her, he said, "What's this about?"

"Are you a cop?"

Dane stayed where he was. The woman was thin, wear-ing only a loose tank top and jeans, and the streetlamps allowed him to see the bruises on her neck and arms. Her long hair looked stringy, dirty. She looked like a feral cat.

"I can get you a cop if you need one."

"Can you get me out of here? There's more of them!"

"Follow me," Dane said.

He didn't reach for her. He just started walking. She fell in step behind him. "I can't believe I found you," she said, still breathless but understandable now.

"What happened?"

"I've been kidnapped," she said. "I was hitchhiking across the country and these guys grabbed me at a bar somewhere in Ohio. They threw me in a van with a few other girls. We were all tied up and drugged."

Dane frowned. He had a feeling he knew where this story was going.

"They said they were going to ship us overseas somewhere," she continued.

"But you got away."

"There are four girls still back at the house!" she said.

"What house?"

"I don't know, couple miles from here? I broke out and just ran."

"Are these men American, foreigners?"

"American."

"Uh-huh."

"Where are we going?"

"Back to my motel room. My girlfriend is there. You can get cleaned up and eat something while we call the cops."

"No, no, skip all that, just get me to the cops. We were going to move on in a few hours."

"Where?"

"A ship at the Port of Wilmington. Do you know where that is?"

"You're in Wilmington."

She gasped.

"What's your name?"

"Wanda."

"Wanda," he said, "I'm Steve Dane."

"And you're not a cop?"

"No, just somebody who knows how to fight the kind of guys you're talking about."

"I loved the way you hit that guy!"

Dane grinned. Cold cocking the punk had indeed felt very good.

And hopefully his prolonged absence would buy them some time.

There were four other women, just like Wanda, to rescue. What bothered Dane was the boldness of the kidnapping. Human traffickers didn't normally grab women from bars. Somebody would miss Wanda; somebody would report her missing. Unless the gang had a plan to get the women out of the country before a search even started. That meant they needed to be deal with. Right away.

And Steve Dane knew how to deal with men like that.

Dane closed the door. Nina was already in bed, on her side, with her back to Dane. She occupied the center of the bed with no room for him. A portable cot sat at the head of the bed.

"I got you a cot," Nina said, without turning to look at him or their guest.

Dane let out a sigh. Now he knew why her Russian intelligence colleagues had called her "Nina the Bitch."

"Get up," he said.

"What did you just say?"

She finally rolled over and sat up and stared at the new arrival. She pulled the neck of her nightgown closed.

"Who is this?"

"Wanda."

"You're picking up strays now?"

"Get up and get dressed, Nina. I'm not telling you again."

"Don't talk to me that way."

He set the bottle down hard on the dresser. With careful words, Dane explained the situation, glancing at Wanda as he spoke, poor Wanda standing by the door with her arms folded, her eyes darting around, as if she'd escaped the frying pan and ended up in the proverbial fire.

Nina's expression changed. She threw the covers off and crossed to the girl, hugging her close. Wanda actually responded, almost melting into Nina, as if a weight had been lifted off her.

"It's okay, honey," she said. "We'll get this straightened

out."

Nina looked Wanda up and down, decided she had a clean outfit that would fit, and quickly tended to the girl, getting her into the bathroom and shower. When Nina emerged, she folded her arms and gave Dane a hard look.

"What's the plan?"

"We call the cops."

"No."

"You have another idea?"

"We find the house and kill some rats. Then we call the cops."

"We only have pistols."

"When has that ever stopped us?"

She pushed past him to take the vodka from the dresser, wiping the blood off on her nightgown. She pulled off the cap and took a long drink.

Dane watched her. Her eyes were alert, but far away.

He said, "What happened in Moscow, Nina?"

She looked at him.

"I'm no stranger to women being smuggled around the world," she said, "and something I did once made the problem worse."

"Really?"

"I didn't know it at the time. I thought what I'd done helped."

Dane waited.

"That's all I'm saying for now," Nina said. "Shouldn't we get the guns out?"

They did.

Chapter Six

Wanda helped Dane and Nina pinpoint the house she'd escaped from with the help of Google Maps. It was only a few miles away in a suburban neighborhood, where the bigger homes sat in front of a forest area sectioned off from the homes to provide the illusion that the owners lived in the quiet countryside. Dane told Wanda to wait in the room till they returned, and he and Nina departed in the rental car.

Presently Dane switched off the lights and guided the car to the curb a few doors down from the target house. The traffickers used a single-level at the end of the street as their safe house, the open space and trees behind the home. In other words, the perfect escape route. It was also the perfect infiltration point.

Dane and Nina walked along the sidewalk. They'd eschewed their usual black combat garb to better blend in, but they were still ready for a fight, Dane with his Detonics Scoremaster .45 stuffed with a ten-round extension magazine, spares behind his back, and a left-over flash-bang stun grenade. Nina packed her compact Smith & Wesson 9-millimeter M&P Shield, having replaced her nightgown with tight jeans and tennis shoes for ease of movement.

Streetlamps lit the way. The houses on either side showed no signs of life at this hour—until Dane passed one fence and woke a dog. Dane and Nina ignored the barking and strode on. When they came abreast of the target house, both dropped behind a car parked on the street. The dog kept barking. The house showed as little life as the rest of the neighborhood. Until the front curtain moved.

A subtle movement, sure, but the kind of quick check a sentry would make in case the barking signaled the arrival of somebody the crew in the house was waiting for, or a police strike team. Which meant something in the house might be worth rescuing.

Two vehicles sat in the driveway, one a small passenger car and the other a large SUV. Crew wagons. Dane and Nina advanced, slid into the shadows on the side of the house and climbed over a gate, the old wood wobbling a little. Landing hard on a concrete path with yard tools to their left, Dane moved forward, staying low, with Nina behind him.

Darkened windows lined the side of the house. When Dane reached the corner, he stopped and scanned the yard. Swimming pool, garden, some trees. A pool of light spilled across a portion of the patio. Shadows moved across the light.

A shovel, rake and smaller pieces of garden equipment lay against the fence to Dane's right. He signaled to Nina, handing her the flash-bang grenade, and grabbed the shovel. He rounded the corner to see the sliding glass doors that provided a partial view of the family room and adjacent kitchen. A man holding a stubby submachine gun was focusing his attention on the family room.

Dane launched the shovel like a spear. He threw high

to compensate for the heavy front end. As the shovel arced and began to descend toward the glass, Dane hauled out the Detonics .45. The metal blade struck the glass low but achieved the desired result. The glass shattered, first in the middle, then spider cracks weakened the rest of the pane. The glass cascaded across the pool of light. Nina pitched the flash-bang, and it exploded within the house, the bright flash and loud bang creating a blinding distraction as the armed man turned with his weapon up. Dane detached the gunman's jaw from his face with a .45 slug.

A woman screamed. Dane and Nina charged through the opening, more glass crunching under them. Dane swung left, right. In the corner of the living room, tied and gagged on the carpet, were four women not unlike Wanda, their wide eyes zeroed in on Dane and Nina.

Nina ran to one, pulled the gag from her mouth.

"Where are the others?"

"It's just us!"

"I mean the bad guys!"

Rubber soles squeaked on the kitchen tile. Dane spun and fired at the gunman, who ducked back. The slug tore a hole in the wall.

"Stay down!" Dane snatched the dead gunner's automatic weapon and jammed the stock into his shoulder. He watched the kitchen and the hallway to the left that led to the front door and living room.

The second gunman rounded the corner ahead, attempting to come down the dark hall, but stopped short. Dane stitched him stomach to chest. The gunman decorated the wall with crimson flecks as he flopped forward onto the carpet.

Dane ran to Nina. Neither she nor the other four women were hurt.

The next part was the hard part, because they had to leave the
women at the house. With no fake identification to show
they were Justice Department agents or affiliated with any
other US federal law enforcement, all they could do was
find a cell phone on one of the dead men and have one of
the women call the police.

Dane and Nina did manage to watch from the car, albeit
parked far enough away that arriving emergency crews
didn't notice them. Presently an ambulance joined the police cruisers, and the women were led out of the house.
Paramedics began checking their condition.

That's when Dane turned to Nina.

"What happened in Moscow?"

"You're like a broken record," she said.

"You aren't responsible, whatever transpired."

"You weren't there."

"Don't you trust me?"

"It's not that." She cleared her throat. "It's hard to
talk about."

Dane waited.

Nina sighed.

"Some gangsters killed my boyfriend, okay? I was
eighteen. When I was old enough, I joined FSB. I wanted
to find out who did it and put them away. Well, I found
out he was part of an investigation into human trafficking
and was on the trail of some big shots who didn't want
to be exposed. Remember Alec Savelev? He helped me
track down the killers, and I ambushed them one night.
Killed all three before they knew what hit them. Problem?
They were part of the smuggling ring, and their removal
let a third party fill the gaps. My little bit of revenge let
the Moscow end of the network connect with a link in

the Balkans to form one of the biggest human trafficking circuits in the world."

Dane let out a breath. "I can see why that would bother you."

"Can you … really? I'm so glad to hear that."

Dane didn't swallow her sarcastic bait. He said, "And after that?"

"You don't want to know about after that," she said.

"Uh-huh."

"So now what?"

Dane tapped a finger on the steering wheel and watched the flashing cherry lights at the house up the street. The cops would be there until way past sunrise. Once the gunmen were identified, the police would summon the FBI. Hopefully then, Dane thought, they could unravel some of the unanswered questions, find the ship Wanda had referred to, maybe save some others already on the ship or arrest the men aboard. But if this incident was part of a bigger network, a global problem, all he and Nina had done was free a couple of victims without really changing the situation.

The thought burned a hole in his belly.

"We continue on to Virginia," Dane said, "and deal with my problem. After that, we need to take up Number One's offer and address your situation."

"I'm not going back to Moscow."

"And I never thought I'd come back to the United States," Dane said, "but it happened. We can't run forever."

"Usually it's me giving lines like that."

"Perhaps you've been a good influence on me."

"Hopefully more than that."

"Of course."

"I'm sorry I didn't tell you."

"I understand."

Dane started the car.

When they returned to the motel, Wanda was gone.

Dane figured it was for the best, and silently wished her luck as he crawled into bed beside Nina. The rollaway cot remained unused.

Chapter Seven

The deepest of the muffled voices on the other side of the wall belonged to Dr. Edward Floyd. What news was he delivering? Or perhaps those patients were not there to hear a death sentence?

Daniel Gallagher sat in a padded chair that wasn't very comfortable, but that wasn't the fault of the person who had done the interior designing. Nothing was comfortable to him anymore. His failing body saw to that.

He waited in the small examining room with its white walls and white-tiled floor and felt a chill through the buttoned-to-the-neck overcoat he wore, which made him look like a tube with skinny legs. He wore the coat so nobody could see how frail he looked, but his face betrayed his true condition, the sunken cheeks, the hollow look in his eyes. Gallagher let his gaze wander around with no real interest. The examining table, with its long paper sheet drawn across the vinyl surface, sat in a corner across from him. When he was a child, those tables had made him nervous, the crinkle of the protective paper he had sat on the stuff of nightmares. The sound was usually followed by an older woman poking him with needles, at least twice. He never knew what the "shots" were for, and he'd been too shy to ask. He was well beyond the need for a shot now, unless they had something in reserve to do what the chemo couldn't.

When the voices on the other side of the wall stopped, Gallagher made a fist with his left hand. Any moment now...

For the longest time the only thing Gallagher heard was the racing of his own heartbeat. When the door finally opened, he jumped. Dr. Floyd, his white coat open, the front pocket loaded with pens, a clipboard in his hand, shut the door.

"'Lo, Dan," he said, pulling over a stool. He sat. He looked at Gallagher and sighed. His eyes never dropped to the clipboard.

"We've done all we can," the doctor said. "I'm truly sorry."

"How long?"

"Six months, max. You might hang on a little longer. I've set up a referral for hospice care. They're expecting your call." Dr. Floyd took a sheet from the clipboard and handed it to Gallagher, who folded it into a pocket. His blank eyes stared past the doctor's right shoulder. He could see Floyd's lips move but didn't really register the other man's face. This conversation was a formality.

"I'll check in on you once a week. We've been through too much for me to leave you alone."

Gallagher finally made eye contact. Dr. Floyd's green eyes blinked. He had a patch of gray at the temples, but the rest of his hair was dark, his face showing the appropriate wrinkles for a man of high education who'd spent his life trying to heal the sick. Gallagher wondered if he should bother with a reply. He knew Dr. Floyd would not be "checking on him" as a service to his oath. The doctor was on Royce's payroll and had his orders. Make sure Gallagher doesn't talk, and silence him if he decides not to die quietly.

He knew there had been similar discussions on San Remo the last two days. He knew Royce and DeRocca were back in the States, but neither had made a move to call him. Of course, that meant they were afraid to talk to him. He didn't blame them. He knew he was a liability, but that didn't mean he agreed with their conclusions.

"Do you have any questions, Dan?"

Gallagher's eyes flashed with defiance. "You tell me I'm dying as if we were talking about buying beer at the grocery store."

"I know. You should have seen the first person I had to tell. A mother of two; she was barely fifty. I didn't feel right for a month after that conversation."

"Was she gone in that time?"

Dr. Floyd nodded.

Gallagher managed a wry smile. "Can you make sure the nurse they send is hot?"

Dr. Floyd managed a laugh.

Gallagher stepped off the bus a few blocks from his apartment and entered a bar.

If he was going to go, he'd go with a drink in his hand. Squeeze a little enjoyment out of his final months.

He let the olive sit for a while in the cold martini. Now with the chemo over, he could at least eat and drink a tiny bit. During the treatments, eating had been something his body didn't want him to do. He shuddered remembering all the time he had spent in the bathroom.

He sat in a corner booth and stared at the drink in between sips.

The bar's lighting was dim, and when the front door opened, the glare from outside flooded the place. Gallagher winced at the bright flash of light. A man with a cane entered. Gallagher watched him in surprise. Perry Royce had decided to show up after all. Perhaps deliver his death sentence firsthand? Sorry, Dan, you know the rules. We can't have you getting delirious and telling secrets. And, course, Royce knew to find him at the bar. Old habits die hard. Just like old men.

Gallagher watched the man approach, the ever-present cane in his right hand. The rubber tip thumped the wood floor. Presently Perry Royce slid into the booth and waved away a waitress.

"What gave me away?" Gallagher said.

"We never escape old habits, and this is the nearest bar to your home."

"What was the verdict in San Remo, Perry?"

"There's no need to get upset."

"I'm not upset, I'd simply like to know if Lassen decided to let me die on my own or have somebody help me along."

"What would you like, Dan?"

"I'd like my old friends to trust me, Perry. That's what I'd like. Less than six months. You can handle that."

"George and I discussed this," Royce said, "and we decided the nurse would be enough security. There's no need for any dramatics here."

"And our friend Cyrus?"

"Don't worry about our friend Cyrus. He's thousands of miles away. It's none of his business. This is between the three of us."

"He'll find out and he'll be pissed you disobeyed."

"There was a time when it was just the three of us. In this instance, it's still the three of us."

"Uh-huh." Gallagher swallowed some of his drink and winced.

"You okay?"

"Everything hurts."

Royce's eyes softened and Gallagher looked away.

"We did some good things, Dan."

"I know we did."

"That's how you'll be remembered."

"You're right behind me, gimpy."

Royce laughed. "There's the Dan I remember. Are you sure you won't make a full recovery?"

"I'm toast." Gallagher took a long drink. "And in a minute, I'm going to be drunk."

Royce stood and extended his hand. Gallagher took it and they shook lightly. Royce's grip was weak, as if he was afraid of crushing Gallagher's hand. "Take it easy."

"Good-bye, Perry."

Royce's sad eyes lingered on Gallagher a moment, then he turned and limped out of the bar with the cane tapping on the wood floor. Gallagher stared at his drink. It wasn't much of a farewell, but they were two old wolves who didn't know any better.

Gallagher didn't blame Perry and George for being worried and discussing his fate with Cyrus Lassen. How many lives had they had snuffed out after similar conversations? Perry and George were all Gallagher had left, and he knew they knew that. His family, long estranged because of his work, didn't even know he was sick. They could read about it in the paper, or wherever obits were printed these days.

Gallagher finished his drink and walked a little un-
steadily out to the bus stop for the short ride home.

They'd done good things, yeah. They'd kept the United
States safe and lined their pockets besides. But there was
that one thing, the one bad thing that had kept him awake
some nights. Just the one.

Chapter Eight

Perry Royce set his cane on the passenger seat and cursed his leg as a stab of pain shot through his calf. Years and years ago Royce had been riding ATVs with friends. He fell off of his. One of his riding buddies, unable to stop in time, ran over his right ankle. Broke it clean and while it healed, as he got older, the injury began causing problems to the point where now he needed a cane and walked with a limp. And it hurt more often than it didn't.

He drove his silver BMW 7 Series into traffic. The dash phone chirped, the words "Unknown Caller" flashing on the center information screen. He pressed a button on the steering wheel to answer. He didn't need to ask who was calling. He already knew.

"Hello, Cyrus."

"You're defying me, Perry. I don't like that."

Perry Royce tried to suppress the chill that crawled up his neck.

"You're spying on me, Cyrus?"

Lassen's chuckle echoed through the car. "Eyes everywhere. How do you think I've survived this long?"

"Gallagher won't talk."

"Dying men always get ideas. They always want to unburden themselves before meeting their Maker. I have sent Miller to DC to deal with the problem. It is now out of your hands."

"That's not necessary."

"Are you going soft on me, Perry?"

"Gallagher and I have been working together a hell of a lot longer than you and I, Cyrus. We owe him."

"We aren't having this argument again. I don't owe him anything. And you work for me."

"At least—"

"No further discussion. Miller will make it look right."

Royce bit off the words he wanted, instead saying, "I guess that's it then."

"Carry on."

"Yes, sir, Cyrus, sir."

A pause on the other end. Then, "Don't get smart with me, Perry."

The line clicked. Royce turned off the dash phone and seethed. Gallagher would die thinking he had lied to him, but there was nothing to be done about it now.

Daniel Gallagher shut the door and froze in place.

The air in the house wasn't right.

Somebody was in his home. Waiting. Royce had lied. Well, no sense prolonging the inevitable.

He walked down the hall to the kitchen with its adjoining family room, where he kept his books, television and a pair of guitars that now had a layer of dust on them. The man on the couch wore a white shirt, a black tie, gray slacks, with a matching coat laid neatly beside him. A leather shoulder holster suspended an unmistakable .45

automatic under his left arm. The man's shoes were mirror bright. His hair was close-cropped, his jawline sharp, his eyes smoldering. A woman stood in the corner. She held a pistol. Unlike the male, she was dressed in jeans with a button-down shirt open to reveal a black tank top, her long black hair tied back. She had the high cheekbones of a Slav and was gorgeous enough to stop traffic. She kept the pistol visible but didn't raise the muzzle.

"Are you here to kill me?"

The man said, "Take off your coat, Daniel."

Gallagher complied and tossed the overcoat on the back of a nearby chair. "I'm not carrying a weapon. I can barely walk."

"Sit down."

Gallagher dropped onto the chair; his breath short. The trip home had exhausted him.

The man took out a cigar and a Zippo and toasted the tip. "My name is Steve Dane," he said. He put the cigar in his mouth and took a puff. Blowing out a stream of white smoke that climbed toward the ceiling, he fixed his gaze on Gallagher and spoke again. "I think you know who I am."

Gallagher's shoulders sank.

Here was the one thing.

Alive.

Steve Dane regarded the frail man silently as smoke trickled from the tip of his San Lotano.

He'd expected to hate the man and he did.

He faced Gallagher with what looked like the same cold calculation with which he'd faced other vermin around the world, but this time it was different. A shot through the head wouldn't suffice. He wanted to make the man suffer.

"Tell me who I am," he said.

Gallagher cleared his throat. He looked a little unsteady. Dane gave him a moment.

Gallagher said, "You're the son of Richard Dane, United States Army veteran and CIA officer."

"That's a good start. What does Richard Dane mean to you?"

"He was a traitor who killed himself."

The woman near the bookcase shifted. Dane held up a hand. Nina Talikova stayed still.

"Wrong answer," Dane said.

"That was the story."

"I came here to learn the truth."

Gallagher eased back in the chair. "What is truth?"

"Pilate said the same thing, as I recall. He was stalling."

Gallagher fixed Dane with a cold stare. "You know as well as I do that the truth only depends on one man lying better than the next."

"I did a job recently," Dane said, turning his attention to his cigar. He took a puff and blew out more smoke. "As a reward, my employer promised to help me solve the mystery of my father's death. They provided your name. I've never believed the suicide story. My father would never betray the US. You might recall I tried to prove that theory."

Gallagher nodded. "I heard."

"And then this happened." Dane clamped the cigar between his teeth and pulled back his right sleeve, revealing puckered, fire-damaged flesh. "A helicopter crash. I've always wondered if there was a connection. Maybe you can fill in the blanks."

Gallagher nodded again.

"You're going to tell me the truth."

"Or what?"

"You're awfully defiant for a man who doesn't have

long to live."

Gallagher choked out a laugh. "You can't threaten to kill me. I'm already dead." His tone softened. "But I'm sorry."

Dane blinked. Nina shifted again.

Gallagher said, "Of all the things we did, what we did to your father bothered me the most."

Dane stared. Frozen. But he started feeling very warm as his heart rate increased. He remained still. Smoke from the cigar drifted in front of his face.

Nina said, "What do you mean?" Her Russian accent sounded thicker with anger.

"Who are you?"

"The one with the gun," she said, raising the pistol. "Answer the question."

Gallagher looked at Dane. "You were sixteen?"

Dane almost whispered. "Yes."

Gallagher nodded. "Your father worked for a man named Perry Royce. Ask around. Legendary spymaster. I worked with him on a project called Operation Eagle. Our job was to sniff out Soviet agents around the world and assassinate them. All hush-hush, look-like-an-accident-type jobs.

"We worked all over the world," Gallagher continued. "It was vital that the Soviets didn't get a foothold in several vital areas, and we kept them at bay. Eagle never saw any press exposure and we avoided Congressional oversight as well. It was one of the most successful secret assassination programs the CIA ever instituted."

"You sound proud."

"I would be allowed to be proud if that's where the killing stopped."

Dane sat straighter. "Where did my father fit in?"

"Royce was a bad egg. He had other ideas when it came to using Eagle. He wanted to work his way into the criminal syndicates and make money on the side, and me and another man named George DeRocca helped him do it. We used agency assets to remove obstacles and filled the voids. Your father found out, and he tried to stop us. We used a Mafia connection to—"

Dane bit down on the cigar, reached for his gun, and removed it from the shoulder leather. The stainless-steel weapon looked large in his hand, larger still because of the extra length of the silencer attached to the muzzle.

"What … what are you doing?"

Dane dropped the San Lotano and stomped it into the carpet. "Royce framed my father?" he asked with deadly calm.

Gallagher started shaking. "He ordered the murder. He also ordered the sabotage of your helicopter. We knew you'd be a problem long before you started asking questions. When you left the US, he decided you weren't a threat anymore. We had a big argument about that. I knew this day would come. I told him you'd never forget. You were simply biding your time."

"Royce was never on my radar." Dane clicked off the .45's safety. It sounded loud in the small room. "I remember DeRocca, though. Came to the house a lot and drank beer with Dad."

"George was second-in-command."

"And what did that make you, Dan?"

"The third man."

Dane rose from the couch and let the .45 dangle in his right hand.

"How long did the doctor give you?"

Nina said, "Steve—"

"Six months."

Dane shot Gallagher's left knee, then his right, the caps popping, splattering blood on the carpet and chair. Gallagher screamed in agony, falling out of the chair to the floor, onto his side. He looked up at Dane with pleading eyes. Dane put a third round through his head, and Gallagher's body jerked with the impact, flopping flat.

Dane jammed his pistol back into the holster. His eyes remained on Gallagher's body; his jaw set tight.

"Why did you kill him?" Nina said.

He looked at her. "In case somebody finds a cure for cancer in the next six months."

"He had more information. Those other two—"

Dane grabbed his coat from the couch and shoved his arms through the sleeves while Nina stared at him.

"He has everything we need," Dane said. "Let's tear this place apart and find the rest. You start upstairs."

Nina put away her gun and brushed by Dane without a word. He heard her feet pound the stairs on the way to the second floor.

He started his meticulous but destructive search with the bookcases, paging through book after book and discarding them on the floor. No hidden computer disks or USB drives.

The pictures on one shelf made him pause. Gallagher's family. Wife. Two kids—boy and girl. There weren't any pictures of mother or kids after the kids were teenagers, so he wondered if at some point they stopped talking to Gallagher. He took one picture down and slid off the back. Nothing hidden there. He dropped the frame, and it landed with a thud. He took the next three, and rage suddenly gripped him like a vise. He pivoted and flung the frames across the room. They smacked into the wall and broke into pieces, the glass shattering, bits raining down on the couch where he'd sat. Jaw clenched tight, breathing hard through his nose, Dane considered the mess momentarily and then moved down the hall to a den, where he found more books and trinkets from Gallagher's life. He tore through everything, wondering if he was truly searching or just making a huge mess reflective of the rage running through him. He tore open the drawers of a desk and dumped out the contents, briefly pawed through the piles. He found a pocket-size spiral notebook with a bunch of words written on each line of each page, one after the other crossed out until he found one that wasn't. Passwords? He pocketed the notebook and then grabbed the laptop sitting atop the desk. Everything he needed was probably on the hard drive. Or maybe there was nothing there. But he wouldn't learn anything by destroying it. He tucked the computer under his arm and started for the hallway, where Nina met him halfway.

"Are you done?" she said.

Dane nodded and led the way to the front door.

"Aren't you going to ask me if I found anything?" she said.

"I don't care," he said, storming out.

Chapter Nine

Killing an old man posed no challenge.

Hal Miller wasn't happy with the assignment from Cyrus Lassen, but he was also in no position to argue. Nobody changed Lassen's mind once he had come to a decision. He'd have had better luck pouring water into the ocean to raise the sea level.

He inched his rental through traffic on his way to a DC suburb where Daniel Gallagher lived. Daniel Gallagher wouldn't live there much longer. He wouldn't live much longer at all, and not because of the cancer ravaging his body.

Miller hadn't always worked for Lassen. His job for a long time was that of enforcer for DC mob boss Gino Moligano, but his skills and talent had impressed Lassen so much, or took Miller on as his own hatchet man. Gino hadn't been happy about that, but he knew arguing with Lassen was useless same as the rest of them, so now Miller followed Lassen's orders and his orders today were to kill an old man and Miller didn't like the idea one bit.

Not because he had any regard for human life but killing

a man who was already dead seemed like a waste of his time and talent.

Orders were orders and all that, so the man wouldn't live to see the sun set.

Traffic inched ahead.

Nina drove while Dane sat in the passenger seat and turned on the computer. As soon as a password prompt appeared, he took out the notebook and found the page with the word that wasn't crossed out. He typed the word and pressed the Enter key. The prompt cleared and showed him the desktop. A beach with a calm ocean served as the wallpaper. How appropriate.

He wasn't conscious of the scenery around him as Nina drove. He clicked on the documents file folder and started scrolling through the contents, presently letting out a low whistle.

"What?" Nina said.

"We got 'em dead to rights," Dane said. "Copies of official mission files going back to the start, and an addendum document detailing the US citizens killed by Eagle operatives."

"Now what?"

"Go back to the hotel so we can finish going through this. If there are still gaps, we'll go see Len Lukavina."

Dane closed the lid and finally looked up. They were at a stoplight and Nina stared at him.

Hal Miller finally turned into the cul-de-sac where Daniel Gallagher lived. Traffic in the DC area was getting worse. Why people continued to put up with the delays and hassles he had no idea. He parked and crossed the street and pulled on a pair of black gloves. He went up the walk to Gallagher's home.

Miller stood tall and trim with slicked-back brown hair and a smooth, chiseled jaw, not a hint of stubble on his face. Even his jeans were perfectly pressed. He had a messy line of work, so he made sure his personal presentation was immaculate at all times.

At the door, he produced lock picks from the inside pocket of his jacket but stopped as he inserted the first into the bottom lock. No resistance. He tried the knob. It was already unlocked. With a quick glance back at the quiet street, he entered the house and shut the door.

No lights. But the smell. The death odor had been building for some time, Miller figured, as he advanced down the hallway. It wasn't hard to find the body. He stopped and stared at the fallen form of Daniel Gallagher and didn't even wrinkle his nose.

He looked around at the ransacking the room had undergone, but ransacking wasn't the right word. Somebody had made a mess. Somebody had wanted to tear the place apart.

His eyes landed on the cigar on the carpet near the couch. The front portion had been flattened into the carpet. He didn't require more proof that somebody else had been here, but the cigar certainly put finality to the point.

Miller took out his phone and snapped a picture of Gallagher's body. He forwarded it to Perry Royce and then called the man. He glanced around at the rest of the room. No sign of forced entry, not even at the front door, but the place had been trashed.

"What is it?" Royce said.

"Gallagher's dead."

"Good."

"Somebody else did it."

"What do you mean?"

"I sent you a picture. It tells the story. Somebody got

here first and put three bullets in him. That same somebody ransacked this house. I can't tell if anything was taken."

"Hang on." Royce muted the line a moment, then came back, his voice more energetic but nowhere near out of control. "Get out of there. We need to know who did this and fast."

"On it," Miller said.

"Leave everything as you found it. I'll send a cleanup crew. We can't have the cops learning about this."

Miller ended the call and returned to his car. He was grinning. Killing an old man might have been a waste of time and effort, but now he had a better mission. Now he had a task worthy of his effort. Who had killed Gallagher? Royce wouldn't have reacted as he had if the killer wasn't a threat to the operation. Any threat to the plan, Miller wanted to stop.

They were all counting on spending the rest of their lives in the safe confines of San Remo.

He drove out of the neighborhood wondering where the trail to the actual killer would lead.

Perry Royce, in the kitchen of his beach home in Manassas, poured a cup of coffee and tried to take a sip, but instead frowned and put the mug on the counter. Leaning against the sink with his arms folded, he dealt with a mix of sadness and dread. Whoever had killed Dan had left a mess. The cleanup crew would take care of the mess, but that still left the mystery of who had shot him and why. It was his number-one priority now.

And then there was the fact that the friend he'd served with for over thirty years was dead. He pushed those feelings away and grabbed the coffee. He hadn't survived this long by letting sentiment blind him, but this was also the first time somebody close to him had been taken out. Ordering the deaths of people you'll never see is one thing; when it's a friend, that's something else. Royce wasn't exactly prepared for "something else," and the hand holding the mug began to shake. He put the mug down again and squeezed his fists tightly. The reaction surprised him, but he couldn't stop shaking.

And all because Lassen couldn't leave well enough alone.

His decision to throw in with Lassen all those years ago was now looking like a grave mistake.

All he'd wanted was money and power. The way to achieve those goals was to carve out one's own empire, and that meant breaking a few skulls. He'd done so, securing a deal with DC mobster Gino Moligano, and that had seemed like his ticket to achievement. But then Lassen showed up and dangled another carrot. It was one thing to have secured a small empire, but what about enjoying a larger one? An empire that came with its own country where Royce and his crew would live out their years in comfort?

Lassen had wanted information in exchange for allowing Royce and his crew into the San Remo scheme. Royce not only had connections with the criminal underworld that Lassen required, but access to intelligence information as well. As a respected member of the CIA alumni, Royce could pass along nuggets that allowed Lassen to continue his own activities free of interference.

Royce wasn't aware of everything Lassen was involved with, but knew the activities included weapons smuggling and the financial backing of jihadist activity. He never asked questions because he hadn't needed to know. Lassen dropped details now and then, and it had been easy to answer questions based on the information Royce passed along, but he'd kept his mouth shut and did his job and made Lassen happy. Lassen, in return, made Royce's bank account happy.

He finally drank some coffee. He decided two could play at the killing game.

Once everything settled down, Lassen might find himself on the wrong end of a gun. Royce and DeRocca could run things in San Remo just fine, thank you very much.

He'd avenge Dan twice.

But he dared not open his mouth in the meantime.

Lassen had eyes and, presumably, ears, everywhere.

Dane sat back and rubbed his face. His head hurt from the glare of the laptop screen despite his turning down the brightness.

Nina sat to his left, nursing a glass of wine. They were in a much better hotel suite than the motel they'd stayed at in Wilmington. Nina had rubbed one of the bathroom towels on her right cheek and pronounced that they were back among the civilized.

Dane scooted his chair back from the corner desk and started to pace.

"What do we know?" he said.

Nina pulled the computer closer to her and consulted the screen.

"We can confirm most of Gallagher's story. US citizens were killed, and they all had Italian names, so it's safe to figure they were the gangsters Gallagher referred to. Their deaths left an opening for Royce and his crew to fill."

Nina made no comment.

"But we don't know who their contact is," Dane continued. "Or was. Who benefitted from those murders? Who got elevated into the big chair because of Royce?"

"We go see Len?"

Dane stopped and nodded. "Let's go see Len."

"It's awfully late, Steve."

Dane glanced at his watch: 2:45 a.m. He hadn't been aware of the passage of time. They'd been at work for hours, breaking for dinner, then back to work.

Dane said, "Then we'll wake him up."

Chapter Ten

Nina watched Dane drive with his hands tight on the wheel and his
focus laser sharp as he watched the road around them. He
breathed deeply through his nose; his mouth closed tightly.
He was seething. She'd never seen him in this state before.

She sat in the passenger seat and let out a sigh. They
hadn't spoken a word since leaving the hotel. She knew
instinctively that anything she tried to tell him would be
met with hostility. He'd made up his mind on what they
needed to do, and they were going to do exactly that, even
if it meant waking up Len Lukavina when they themselves
should have been in bed.

She faced forward as passing streetlamps flashed
brief bursts of illumination into the car. There was no
reaching him in this current state. His obsession with
answers was finally coming to the surface, and how long
had it been simmering? Long enough. Long enough indeed. Maybe she should cut him the slack he'd not allowed her in Wilmington.

She wasn't blind to the similarities between them.
Instead of expressing her rage at what had happened in

Moscow, she turned inward and refused to talk. Dane was expressing outwardly, and maybe talking too much, and certainly not going about this personal mission (there was no other word for it) with the concentration of missions in the past.

He was going to make a mistake, hurt himself; hurt her; hurt somebody.

She'd be a hypocrite if she said anything, but how could she not?

But now was not the time. Not when he was on fire with rage. Maybe Lukavina would set him straight. Dane needed somebody to yell at him, bring him back to reality. Nina didn't think she was the person to do that.

"Dammit, Steve!"

"I wouldn't be here this late if it wasn't urgent. We need to talk. Right now."

Dane, with Nina slightly behind him, stood in the entryway of Len Lukavina's home in Arlington. Lukavina's wife stood near her husband. Both were in bathrobes, with sleepy eyes.

At forty-six, a few years older than Dane, Lukavina had moved up the ladder at the Central Intelligence Agency despite an almost fatal accident. One side of his face appeared warped. The corner of one eye drooped, and the lid didn't move when he blinked. Lukavina had been one of the agents on Steve Dane's Black Hawk helicopter when it crashed, and he was one of the last Dane had pulled out of the wreckage before the chopper exploded. Lukavina took the most punishing blast of the explosion, nearly burning to death. The damage had been so extensive that no amount of plastic surgery could fully erase the effects. The incident forced him to remain behind the scenes, even when in the field running other agents, until a recent promotion to director of the agency's counter-terrorist division. He didn't like riding a desk, but he appreciated the ability to still function in some capacity.

Dane always felt a twinge of guilt when he saw Len. Not that he couldn't have saved him sooner, but that Dane was scarred less. Dane could cover evidence of his injury with long-sleeved shirts. Lukavina had no such option.

Lukavina and Dane stared at each other for a moment. Then Lukavina said, "All right." His wife told him not to take too long and went back upstairs.

Not the reaction Nina wanted.

She remained quiet and followed Dane and Lukavina across the living room to a small office with a desk and chairs, bookcases and no mementos of his CIA work. There were pictures of him in his Marine Corps uniform and of his family. A silent desktop computer sat on the very clean desk.

Lukavina sat behind his desk. Nina took a seat in front, but Dane remained standing, starting to pace as he spoke. He told his friend everything about Daniel Gallagher, the files on the murder victims, all of it. He finally stopped talking and pacing once he reached the end of the tale.

The CIA man sat stunned. Finally, he said, "Wow."

"We need to compare what we have with what's in the agency archives. I want to know how they covered up the unauthorized killings. I'd also like to know where Royce and DeRocca are now."

Lukavina, his face twisted in thought, fired up his computer. "I can access the headquarters server," he said, "so we should be able to find something. But the agency doesn't necessarily keep track of retired staff. Royce and DeRocca could be anywhere."

Dane started pacing again, ignoring a concerned glance from Nina. A few minutes later Lukavina said, "Got it."

Dane moved behind the desk and leaned over Lukavina's chair.

"The file's locked up tighter than a nun's you-know-what," the CIA man said.

"That's gross, Len," Nina said.

"What it means is that I can't access the file remotely."

Dane moved around the desk again. "Can you try in the morning?"

"During lunch, sure. This is huge though, Steve. Royce and DeRocca and Gallagher are legends. And they may still have friends keeping an eye on this. We have to be careful."

"We need to find them."

"Your shooting Gallagher will get the cops involved, you realize."

"And the cops can work for us, too."

"What do you mean?" Lukavina said.

"Talk to them and suggest it might be a Mafia killing. Get them sniffing around. It'll spook Royce and make him send somebody after us."

"You can't be serious."

"If you can't find Royce directly, the mob connection is our next best bet."

"I'm going to need some time, Steve. And I think you need some sleep."

"Preach it," Nina said.

"What I need is action, Len, not stalling."

"Who's stalling? I want to help. But I need time. You have to remember the agency has rules. The law says we can't work domestically. If anybody gets any hint that I'm snooping around in what is not in any way agency business—"

"All right," Dane snapped.

Lukavina fell silent.

Dane moved around the room, his hands behind his back.

"Where are you staying?" Lukavina said.

"The Watergate," Nina said.

Lukavina showed Dane and Nina to the door and saw them out. Dane stopped on the front step and turned around.

"I appreciate everything, Len."

"I know you do. This is my fight, too. Don't forget that."

"I won't."

Dane shut the door of their hotel room, and Nina made a beeline for the dresser, where a bottle of wine sat. She started working out the cork.

Dane stopped her, took the bottle and popped the cork. Then he pivoted to the bathroom and poured the bottle out in the sink.

"Hey!" Nina stopped in the doorway as the bottle went glug glug glug. "You're wasting my vitamins!"

"I need you sober for this one."

"You what?"

"Sober," Dane said, shaking out the last drops. "As in, not drunk."

"Why are you suddenly no fun?"

"Just this once, honey. Seriously."

He dropped the bottle in the trash, where it hit so hard that the small wastebasket fell over and the bottle rolled across the tiled floor. Dane squatted down to put it right and placed the bottle at the bottom. Nina moved out of the doorway and let him pass. Dane removed his suit jacket and draped it across a chair, removed his tie and his shoes.

"That means me, too," he said, digging out a pint of Jack Daniel's from a shoulder bag under the writing table.

He tossed it to her. She twisted off the top and poured it down the drain. Returning from the bathroom, she said:

"Somehow I don't think I'm even."

"This is the big one, babe. Our usual shenanigans have no place here. We need to stay focused."

"What aren't you saying in all this?" Nina said, folding her arms.

Dane looked at her. She hadn't said much since Gallagher's. He figured there was a lot she wanted to say, but it was simmering beneath the surface.

"I almost killed the wrong man a long time ago."

"What do you mean?"

"I had it all wrong."

"Tell me."

"My father once worked as part of a joint FBI and agency team that found a Russian sleeper cell in the US. Dad worked the overseas angle. He's the one who found them, and the bureau made the arrests. I always thought it was them who killed him—one in particular named Rosov. It made sense. Get revenge against the man who found you by making him look like a traitor. I was about to go to Russia and shoot him, but Peter Cross stopped me."

"Before or after he became president?"

"Before. He was still at CIA and so was I. He convinced me there wasn't enough evidence, but I didn't believe him at the time. I still agreed to wait until more proof was available. It drove me nuts. Crazy with rage, Nina.

"Then the helicopter crash happened and almost killed me and Len. I couldn't get control of myself. That's when I hit the road. Quit CIA, quit everything."

Nina's face softened, but she offered no reply.

"There isn't any room for mistakes this time."

"Yet you just blasted Gallagher like swatting a fly,"

she said. "Was that a mistake?"

"He'd served his purpose."

"Let's just say I saw some of the rage you refer to, and if you go overboard, you'll ruin your chances of clearing your father's name, and you might ruin everything between us."

"What does that mean?"

"You'll be dead, or I'll be dead. Get your head straight."

"Why do you think I'm getting rid of the booze?" he said. "I wouldn't undo shooting Gallagher, but I might prefer a different frame of mind when I shoot the next one."

She moved closer to him, and in a soft voice said, "Do you think Cross knew something you didn't? Otherwise why tell you Rosov wasn't guilty?"

Dane froze a moment, then took a deep breath. "I never asked myself that," he said. "I didn't even stop to think. I just took off with my tail between my legs."

"Sounds like you and him need to talk."

"You bet we will."

"First we need to follow Len's advice and get some rest." She closed the distance between them and started undoing the buttons on his shirt. "I mean it, Steve. It will wait until morning."

Dane pulled her close and rested his face in her neck as she continued undressing him. What he wanted to say was that she was the one who had finally pulled him out of the personal hell he'd been living in, finally made it okay for him to live again and find a new purpose.

When he left the CIA, there was nothing to do except find a way to make a living using his unique skill set. The 30-30 mercenary unit had filled that role for a while. He took charge of his life as best as he could and tried to forge a new destiny despite the cloud of anger hanging over him. A skirmish in South Africa netted several million dollars' worth of diamonds that would sustain him, and he disbanded the unit.

After that, he was a knight errant in the service of those who needed a champion, bringing the fight to the predators who sought to exploit the defenseless, because he needed to be the champion that hadn't been there for him.

Somewhere along the way, the beautiful creature in his arms entered his life and made him feel again.

And now he realized he had been, the whole time, fighting for himself.

Someday he'd find the right words and tell her.

Or maybe she already knew.

Chapter Eleven

Dane snored.

Nina lay awake counting spots on the ceiling. You'd
think they'd have cleaned the spots off the ceiling and how
the heck did they get up there anyway?

He at least knew what his problem was, she realized.
Part of his rage came from making a mistake he'd have
never been able to correct. It made her feel a little better,
that at least he knew to watch his steps now, but still. . .

She knew she had to sleep. She'd advocated for sleep,
but that was before Dane dumped her booze. The only
thing that waited in her slumber were nightmares. And if
Dane continued on his path and didn't correct his course,
she might lose him too. That's what worried her the most.
Sure, he wanted to remain sober, better focused, but his
face during their discussion betrayed nothing but rage she
wasn't sure he could control.

She had to do everything possible to keep Steve from
going over the edge while not stopping him from achieving
his goal. That meant honoring his request and not sneaking
out for liquor. He slept so deeply, he wouldn't hear her

leave or come back. She could have come and gone already. Maybe it was time for her to try life without booze. As she'd realized in Wilmington, her "vitamins" didn't help chase away the nightmares.

The booze might have made them worse.

She turned on her side and closed her eyes and tried to get some rest.

Cyrus Lassen didn't doubt for one minute that his time in San Remo could be cut short if he and President Marco had a falling out of any kind, so Lassen employed a strategy that had always served him well: keep your client happy.

In the case of President Marco, Lassen traveled to the presidential mansion once a week for whiskey and darts with the leader of San Remo.

Diego Marco, long before taking charge of the small Central American country, had attended college in the United States, where he'd become an avid player of darts, sometimes missing classes for take part in various tournaments. He'd brought the hobby home with him, but he had no real competition to play against. He could teach people all day, but he still beat them.

And then Lassen showed up.

Skill with darts was only part of Lassen's resume. He'd learned to throw darts with precision same as he'd learned to throw knives and to swing swords.

As the chief of his house guard, Sanchez, drove Lassen onto the presidential palace property, Lassen reflected that the building wasn't as nice as the retreat he occupied. The complex sat in the middle of the Capitol city, so all San Remo citizens could marvel over the great minds that occupied the building.

The rebels probably wouldn't look at it that way, but

that was the working theory.

San Remo had not been at war when Cyrus Lassen first approached President Marco with his idea of turning the country into a sanctuary for people who needed a place to hide as long as they had an ability to pay.

Marco had loved the idea of being a beacon of hope to the hopeless. As he and Lassen discussed the project further, Marco began having grand visions. Luxury hotels, private residences, casinos, a wide variety of entertainment, all engineered to keep their wealthy and of course low-profile clients happy as they enjoyed the sanctuary offered by El Presidente Diego Marco.

Lassen agreed he was a visionary indeed. Marco liked compliments.

Keep your client happy.

The war had started after Marco decided to jail an activist college teacher named Fernando Gomez. Mr. Gomez began writing articles for the opposition newspaper listing Marco's human rights violations and his increasing totalitarianism and its effect on the San Remo population. These articles stirred heavy debate and protest on both sides, because most of the population was perfectly fine with the benevolent dictatorship of Diego Marco.

It was only those who stood in the way of progress and wound up in prison and labor camps that objected to him, Marco declared. And if they all learned to go along and get along, there wouldn't be any problem.

The story didn't end there, and Gomez continued his writings, and protests against the Marco government increased, and soon the president had no choice but to crack down on the demonstrators because they were interfering with the everyday business of the nation.

When one such protest ended in scores of deaths at

the hands of the San Remo army, Gomez and his "Sons of San Remo" began to form. The war started in earnest when assassins killed Fernando Gomez during a speech. His sons, Roberto and Rico, took over leadership of the Sons and fought hard in response.

But they were inexperienced fighters which the San Remo army proved time and again.

They remained a threat as long as they existed, however. Somebody might teach them how to fight. Somebody might show up to organize their efforts better.

Until they were dead and gone, there would be no rest in San Remo.

Despite the crisis, President Marco insisted on playing darts once a week with Cyrus Lassen.

Sanchez parked the car in front of the main building and an armed military escort, one sergeant, brought Lassen to President Marco's office.

"Welcome, Cyrus, welcome, my friend!" The portly president came around his desk with his arms out. Lassen returned the hug. He was almost three feet taller than Marco, and his rotund form made him look like a potato next to the slender Lassen.

"Drink?" Marco guided Lassen to the bar on the wall. "Your usual?"

"Sure," Lassen said.

Normally Marco had an assistant pour the drinks, but Marco wasn't on duty right now. He was with a pal. Lassen glanced around the wood-paneled office with its basic furnishings and once again decided it could have fit right in with any midlevel manager office in America circa 1973. Marco seemed to insist on his office being a time capsule.

The dart board hung on the far wall to Lassen's right.

"How are things progressing?" Marco put ice in two glasses and filled one with Jack Daniels. "I understand you had two of your American associates visit recently."

Lassen grinned. Of course, the president knew. As Marco handed him a glass, Lassen described his meeting with Royce and DeRocca.

"Everything still on track?" Marco said.

"We'll be ready as soon as the rebels are dealt with, Mr. President."

Marco swallowed a gulp of whiskey. "I was thinking about that very thing. You know they call you the Gringo Dragon, right?"

Lassen laughed. "No."

"We picked up that phrase from a couple of rebels in the city we captured," Marco said. "Anyway, wouldn't it be nice to try and capture one of the Gomez brothers?"

"I like where this is going."

"You take lunch on the balcony every day, don't you?"

"Are you spying on me, Mr. President?"

Diego Marco laughed heartily as he moved to the dart board and began pulling darts out of the target. "We have eyes and ears everywhere, my friend, you know how it is. Anyway, I was thinking, if word leaked to the rebels that this was your routine, and one of the Gomez brothers showed up with a team to try and kill you, well, that might make a good capture, help end the fight, don't you think?"

"Sure."

"You could make an example out of him, right?"

"Won't be hard."

"Then let's play darts," President Marco said, "and talk about how we might work this out."

"It assumes one of the Gomez brothers will show up."

Marco laughed. "I had their father shot. They know you're important to the machinations here in San Remo. If they get a chance at your neck, one of them will show up."

Lassen decided not to argue. Marco was a politician. Politicians knew everything. And he beat the rotund man at darts without regret.

Chapter Twelve

Gino Moligano lived in a white mansion on the southern side of DC, a stone's throw from Fort Washington. It was the largest home in the area, surrounded by a wrought iron fence, and in the middle of a lush green field. Cameras, armed security guards, warning signs—the works. It kept people at bay. The blue sky and green hills made it an ideal place.

Moligano waited on his terrace with a strong sense of frustration and irritability. He knew all about the trip Perry Royce and George DeRocca had made to San Remo, albeit the decision made about Gallagher didn't bother him—he hadn't known the man. What did bother him is that he was left out. Over time, he'd fallen further down the totem pole.

The marble terrace with its Romanesque railing over-looked the capo's large, blooming garden. Unseen birds chirped. Moligano was going gray at the temples, but the rest of him looked like he could go a few rounds in the ring. He had started as a boxer, gotten in with the so-called bad crowd and worked his way up through the organization. He sat in the seat of power because Perry Royce had cleared the way with the bullets of more than one assassin. He owed the man, but loyalty only went so far when they left him out of the discussion process.

He swallowed more of his gin and tonic and wondered if he should be so upset. When Lassen and President Marco finally properly set up San Remo, he'd have a place to retire to.

No, what really steamed him up was that he'd been told to be ready for a visit from Hal Miller, the contract killer. There was a time when Miller had been his subordinate. Lassen took a liking to the guy and brought him to his end of the triangle. Now the son of a bitch thought he was a big shot.

One of the house guards stuck his head out the balcony doors.

"Miller's here, sir."

"Uh-huh," the gangster said.

The guard didn't leave.

"What's wrong?"

"There was some trouble at the gate. A mix-up. We turned him away at first."

Moligano laughed. "Did that make him mad?"

"Very mad."

"Good work. Send him up."

The challenge at the gate, a few minutes earlier, had almost resulted in Hal Miller shooting a bunch of guys.

Miller steered the Cadillac onto the short driveway approaching the main entrance of the Moligano home. The grounds appeared as immaculate as ever. One thing Molgano insisted on was proper landscaping.

A guard stepped out of a shack. His shirt strained against a pot belly, and a revolver hung below his left arm. He held out a hand. Miller stopped the car and rolled down the window.

"Tell Gino that Miller is here."

"He's not seeing anybody."

"He'll see me."

"I got my orders. Beat it."

"Don't make me get out of this car."

The guard stepped back and yanked his radio and took out the revolver. Miller bolted from the car. The guard started talking into the radio and swung the gun up at the same time. Miller grabbed the gun, twisted, forcing the guard's body to turn with the twist, and socked him in the mouth with his free hand. The guard dropped onto his rear. The radio clattered beside him. Miller was ejecting the shells from the revolver as more guards ran toward him.

Each of them held a weapon on Miller from the other side of the fence. The man in charge, a trim fellow this time, stepped forward. "What's the idea, Miller? Gino ain't seeing anybody."

"Will you ask him already? Tell him Royce sent me."

"You can tell me."

"Get your boss down here or we're going to piss off the neighbors with a lot of shooting." Miller opened his coat and took out his Glock-21 automatic. He kept it beside his leg as he scanned each face of the men before him. One or two started looking nervous and tightened the grips on their own weapons.

The shack guard moaned a little.

"Everybody take it easy," the trim guard said. He took out his radio and spoke to somebody about Miller. After a short wait and a positive response, he told his guys to scoot, opened the gate and told Miller to drive up to the front of the house.

Miller put his gun away and followed directions.

Not like he needed them. He already knew the way. He found Moligano on the balcony sipping a gin and tonic.

"I would have liked watching you try to gun down my men, Hal."

"Maybe next time," Miller said with a cocky grin.

Moligano took a seat at a glass table. The metal chairs all had a cushion on the seat that was tied to the back. Before Miller sat, he brushed the cushion with a handkerchief. Folding the cloth, he returned it to his back pocket and joined the older man. Moligano downed what remained of the gin and tonic and told Miller's escort to bring them a couple of beers. When the beers arrived and the escort departed, Moligano took a long drink.

Miller examined his bottle. It was a little early to start drinking, but what the heck. He swallowed a mouthful.

"What does Perry need?" Moligano said.

"Don't sound so excited."

"It's hard not giving the orders."

"We have a problem, some unknown shooters," and Miller filled in the capo on the details surrounding Gallagher's murder. "We're stumped," he said in conclusion.

"Wasn't one of my people," the capo said.

"We aren't suggesting it was," Miller said. "Whoever did it, we need help tracking them down. I can't cover the territory alone."

"But you have nothing to go on."

"Right."

"I'm not sending men out on a wild-goose chase. Find me a target and I'll give you all the guys you need."

"I just said—"

"I'm not in the mood to repeat myself, Hal."

Miller was not about to give up so easily. "Whoever killed Gallagher, whatever they want, they may find a connection to you."

"Good. We'll take them out when they try to hit me. What's the problem?"

Miller glared at the capo. "It's not a sound strategy."

"You got your ways; I got mine."

Miller rose from the table. "I didn't come here for an argument."

"I'm just telling you my position. Tell me you have a lead and I may change my mind."

"I don't."

"Then my decision stands until new information comes in."

"I understand."

"If Royce has any questions—"

"He'll call you." Miller started for the exit. "I'll find my own way out."

"Don't kill any of my guys," Moligano said. "I understand the way things are now, but if you take things too far, you'll be shown the hard way who still holds the power in this town."

"Think you'll get away with it?"

"Don't let the gray hair fool you. Beat it."

Miller stayed a moment, watching Moligano stew in his chair. The capo knew he was there, but pretended he wasn't. Then the killer quietly departed. Moligano let out a sigh.

Chapter Thirteen

Andy Swindol had never attracted the right kind of attention.

He was a slight man, fair haired, his clothes never quite fit properly, especially the suit he was expected to wear to work at the Central Intelligence Agency.

He worked in Records. He was The Keeper of Secrets. The rows and rows of hard-copy files, and server upon server loaded with digital files, all under the watch of he and his staff. He felt it gave him some importance, though he knew he'd never be promoted anywhere else in the Company and certainly wouldn't earn an overseas posting. He wasn't case officer material. He wasn't an agent, the term he preferred, in any way, shape or form.

Which made him a perfect recruit for Perry Royce. As the man who knew the secrets, his job was to tip off Royce if the wrong people started sniffing through those secrets, and provide answers to questions Royce asked from time to time, usually details of on-going efforts that the old spymaster used for purposes Swindol had no business asking about. For the service, Royce paid handsomely. That's all that mattered.

Swindol hadn't had the family connections that a lot of upper-level CIA people had, such as Royce. While he'd gone to a good school, he has no Skull-And-Bones affiliation, and none of the fraternal connections. He'd impressed the recruiters and interview staff with his knowledge, ability and degrees; they assigned him to Records.

Swindol sat at his desk reviewing information on his screen that advised him of who accessed what the day before. Standard security check. Can't have people with the wrong access trying to read a file they had no business reading.

The last notation made him sit up in his chair.

The last notation made him quickly call Perry Royce.

It wasn't the first time an early-morning call had woken Perry Royce from a sound sleep.

Royce rolled over in the empty bed and picked up the phone.

"Yes?"

"It's Swindol."

"What is it?"

"Somebody tried to access the Eagle files last night."

"Who?"

"Leonard Lukavina, head of the counter-terrorist unit."

Royce swung his legs over the side of the bed, sitting up sharply. His ankle flared and he bit off a grunt. "Why?"

"No idea. It was a quick query, he was denied, and he logged off."

Lukavina would have no business looking at those files. Nobody had any business looking at those sealed and buried files, but considering what had happened to Gallagher, Royce knew the query was no coincidence.

And if they were looking for the official file, maybe

they hadn't found anything at Gallagher's after all.

Which meant the CIA might have been behind Gallagher's death.

"I'll take care of it," Royce said. "Thanks for calling."

"It's what you pay me fore, sir."

"Keep earning that pay."

Royce set the phone down and rubbed his face. He picked up the phone again and called Hal Miller. After the assassin updated Royce on his visit with Moligano, Royce told him about the new lead. "Stay with Lukavina until we know who he's working with. I guarantee you that's our connection."

"On it," Miller said.

The elevator doors dinged open and Len Lukavina stepped into the outer office of the CIA's director.

It wasn't his first summons to the office on the seventh floor, but it wasn't scheduled, and Lukavina wondered if his attempt at accessing a classified file had anything to do with the sudden request to see the director.

While he might have to explain what he was doing, Lukavina knew he had a sympathetic ear in Carlton Figg. The DCI would listen fairly.

Pumped up with three cups of coffee, Lukavina crossed the carpet to the desk of the DCI's secretary who said good morning and announced his arrival. Lukavina shut the inner-office door behind him.

Figg, in a dark suit, his full head of hair a light gray, stood by the panoramic window overlooking the Virginia hills in the distance.

"Good morning, Len."

"Hello, sir." Lukavina stood and waited to be invited to sit.

Figg turned and approached his desk, which sat in front of a wall bearing the CIA seal bookended by American flags. Figg gestured to a seat. Lukavina sat.

"I hear you were snooping around last night," Figg said. "Looking into Operation Eagle. You don't have any reason for doing that, Len. It's not related to counter-terrorist activity. What's going on?"

"I was doing a favor for a friend."

Figg raised an eyebrow. "I don't like where this is going."

"The friend is Steve Dane."

"Now I really don't like where this is going. Steve Dane left this agency long ago and should not be a concern of yours."

"What if I told you he had information that the people in charge of Operation Eagle used it for illegal purposes?"

Figg placed his elbows on the armrests of his chair and made a tent with his fingers. "Tell me more."

Lukavina explained about Gallagher's information, and left out nothing that Dane had confided, including the murders on US soil. That information sobered Figg greatly, it seemed.

"As I recall, sir, you knew Dane's father."

Figg nodded. "I did."

"I think we should give Dane whatever aid he needs."

"Do you realize what you're suggesting?"

"Yes, sir. But look at it this way. If we let Dane investigate for us, we're in a better position to keep it quiet. The last thing we need is any friends Royce and DeRocca still have here, and we know they do, tipping them off."

"Why haven't the police been in touch about Gallagher's body?"

"Excuse me, sir?"

"If the police had found Gallagher's body, we would

have been called. We haven't been."

Lukavina frowned. "I'd have to check the house myself, sir. Maybe the neighbors haven't noticed anything untoward."

"Either that or our friends are cleaning up the trail. That means Steve is in danger. That means you are vulnerable, too. You mentioned Royce's friends. Records reported what you had done, so I'm not the only one who may know you tried to access that file."

"It's your decision, sir. Do we help Dane or not?"

"It's hard to believe that story, but I don't think Gallagher would make it up, either."

Lukavina nodded.

"And Dane has proof on the laptop?"

"Yes, sir."

"Let's go with it for now," Figg said. "We'll re-evaluate as more information comes to light. If Dane is right, we have a serious problem. If he's wrong, we need to cut him off right away."

"If he's wrong, I don't think he'll make trouble, sir."

"Steve Dane has been making trouble ever since he left this agency."

"Sometimes that trouble has helped us, sir."

Figg smiled. "Which is why I'm not upset about it. Carry on, Len. Go see what happened at Gallagher's and keep me posted."

Lukavina left the DCI's office feeling better than when he'd arrived.

Chapter Fourteen

Lukavina held his morning staff meeting and listened to the updates on various assignments while, silently, he plotted out his own activities. After the meeting ended, he announced to his secretary that the director had some tasks for him, and he'd be out of the office the rest of the day but always accessible via cell.

Lukavina made his way to Gallagher's home but wasn't taking anything for granted. He didn't drive a direct route and made U-turns to backtrack several times. No sign of any surveillance. When he reached Gallagher's neighborhood, he made a circle in the quiet cul-de-sac and parked the car in front of Gallagher's yard. Nothing at the front of the house seemed disturbed. Lukavina went up to the front door to find it locked. Lukavina crossed the driveway to the side of the house and took a deep breath as he examined the fence blocking his way to the back of the house. He could step on the water meter, hop over and land on the other side. But could he do it without ruining his suit? This was the kind of covert stuff he'd been forced to give up. He smiled at the opportunity.

He planted one foot on the water meter, planted both hands on the top of the fence and boosted his body up and over. He landed hard on the other side, a sharp pain flashing up each leg. He leaned against the outer wall of the house a moment. Ouch indeed. He didn't have the shoes for this either. Or, more likely, he wasn't in shape for this. You're just getting old. He brushed off his suit. No rips or tears. Good.

He walked along the side of the house. Yard equipment sat against the wall, the trash cans covered, no flies evident. He made it to the backyard. Still nothing out of place. Moving around to the back-patio doors, he cupped his hands over his eyes and looked in. Dane had said the room just in front of the patio doors was where he and Nina had had their chat with Gallagher. The room looked spotless and, frankly, unlived in, almost too clean. None of the mess Dane had described, or the body, remained.

The police hadn't contacted the agency about the murder of a retired employee because they hadn't found the victim to begin with.

Lukavina hopped the fence again and returned to his car. As he drove away, he dialed Dane's cell.

"Where are you?" the CIA man said.

"At the hotel."

"I have some news." Lukavina updated Dane about Gallagher's missing body. "Which means they're looking for you," he concluded.

"Good."

"I have an idea that might move things along a little bit."

"I'm listening," Dane said.

"I'm on my way to meet a cop friend. He's one of our regular sources. I'll ask him who benefitted from an arrangement with Royce."

"We'll stay here till you call back."

"You sound awfully mellow, Steve."

"I needed a reality check, and I got one. Thanks, Len."

Lukavina hung up and presently he parked curbside near a coffee shop, where some patrons were sitting outside. One in particular wore a blue shirt and black slacks, his white hair combed straight back, a string tie down the front of his shirt. He had a wiry runner's body and was reading on an iPad.

Lukavina approached. The man looked up and smiled, stood with an offered hand.

"Len, good to see you again," said Detective Sergeant John Bishop.

"Likewise."

"I got you a regular," Bishop said as they sat, gesturing to the second cup of coffee on the table.

Lukavina took a drink. "Very good. I hope my text wasn't too vague."

Bishop closed the tablet's cover. "Why don't you tell me what's up?"

Lukavina scooted his chair closer. "We're looking at a corruption case, some of our own people getting in deep with the mob."

"Very interesting."

"We have part of the story but not all of it, and you've been with the department long enough that we can probably put some stray chapters together."

"Okay."

"Think back over the last twenty years, maybe more," Lukavina said. "We know the mob has a D.C. element. Were there any major killings of important people in that time, and who would have benefitted?"

Bishop let out a whistle.

"And the people you're investigating filled the gap created by those murders?"

"Exactly."

Bishop sat back, folded his arms and thought for a moment. Lukavina watched him, almost tuning out the street sounds and other activity around him.

"Well, everybody talks about Gino Moligano," Bishop said.

"Who's he?"

"He was nobody twenty years ago, but he's the big boss of D.C. today. He got there when his boss, and most of his boss's lieutenants, were killed. Actually, they had accidents, very convenient accidents."

"And the murders remain unsolved?"

"We couldn't prove they were murders," Bishop said. "And it's hard to say we cared about a bunch of gangsters blowing themselves away. As long as civilians weren't hurt."

"The top bosses in New York didn't step in?"

"Oh, they did. They sent somebody to make sure the violence stopped. That's when Moligano was crowned big boss. We don't know what kind of deal they made, but there were no more accidents."

"And he's been untouchable ever since?"

Bishop nodded. "The FBI has tried to get him on a RICO charge many times, but there was always interference. I mean big interference, Len. Protection from Satan himself."

"It's a place to start."

"I don't wanna know what you do next."

"Yes, you do," Lukavina said.

"Yes, I do. But I don't. Get it?"

"Thanks for the coffee, John." Lukavina picked up his cup and shook Bishop's hand before leaving.

Hal Miller watched the exchange between Lukavina and Bishop from across the street.

Royce had supplied a picture and an address for Lukavina via their man Swindol at CIA. It wasn't hard to pick up his trail from his home and follow him around. For a former field man, he'd become very sloppy. His surveillance evasion, a few turns here and there while driving, was easy to defeat.

He didn't follow Lukavina as he left the coffee shop but called Royce instead.

"He talked to somebody. A cop, I think."

"About what?"

"I wasn't close enough to hear. Short chat. Probably just asked a few questions."

"We have to assume they're going to be onto us soon."

"Should I take him out?"

"No. Not yet. I want the one he's working for. Let's put Gino on alert."

"Okay."

Miller started the car and drove away.

Chapter Fifteen

Dane waited alone.

The meeting he'd arranged earlier for the evening was between him and one other man only. Nina remained at the hotel, where she swore up one side and down the other that she would not go out and buy a bottle of wine or any other alcoholic beverage, but she probably had already done so out of spite. It wasn't like he could do anything to stop her, but maybe for once she'd understand the importance of his wishes and remain sober. He'd see for sure when he returned.

He stood under a streetlamp in a quiet business park in Dupont Circle, the sky dark, the chill of the night biting through his suit jacket. He was unarmed and felt naked.

A black Town Car turned the left corner, and the bright headlamps illuminated him. He didn't raise an arm to block the glare. The car pulled over and stopped. Nobody exited. Dane approached the rear passenger-side door and climbed inside, settling on the plush leather seat and snapping his seat belt as the driver, without a word, accelerated away. Dane placed his hands on his lap and stared ahead. The outside scenery held no interest.

The Town Car pulled into the rear entrance of the White House, where Secret Service agents put Dane through their security protocols, which included a body scan, a pat-down, a retinal scan and visual confirmation from the chief of staff. The chief of staff then escorted Dane through the quiet hallways to the Oval Office, where President Peter Cross waited. The president thanked the chief of staff, who left them alone, closing the office door quietly.

Cross stood tall behind the big oak desk, where his predecessors had made tough calls and major decisions affecting millions. He smiled at Dane and came around with a hand extended; Dane met him halfway and they shook, the handshake turning into a hug.

"I can't believe how long it's been," Cross said. "You look well, Steve."

"And you, sir," Dane said. He took a deep breath. "You probably know why I'm here."

"I've been waiting a long time for this meeting."

Dane followed Cross's invitation to sit, and the president resumed his position behind the desk. As soon as he sat down his face looked tired, worn out. Cross and Dane had known each other for two decades. Cross had been in charge of Special Activities at CIA and later rose to the DCI position prior to entering politics, enjoying a short congressional career and ultimately winning the presidency.

Despite Dane's attempt to sever links with his past, Cross remained somebody he could never fully abandon. He had known Cross as a tough but fair boss who always looked after his operatives and had taken a vested interest in the case of Dane's father. Dane knew Cross and his father had not been close, but they'd worked on projects together, and Cross felt from the get-go that something about Richard Dane's death seemed false when other agency officials rushed to embrace the treason story.

"Been a long couple of weeks," Cross said, "but nothing compared to what I'm sure you're going through."

"As usual, sir, it sounds like you're a few steps ahead."

"It's not a mistake that the Trust found you," the president said. "We've been waiting for events to accelerate to the point where we could bring you fully up-to-date and finish this."

Dane frowned.

"I've known Daniel Gallagher was sick for a long time. He was the weak link in Royce's chain, but without his death sentence we couldn't have reached him. Once we knew he could be broken—"

"You've known all this time? The whole story?"

Cross raised a hand. "Stephen, the last time we spoke about this, you were hurt and angry and ready to murder a man who had nothing to do with your father's death. You weren't ready then."

"It might have been nice to make that choice myself."

"Even if I had told you, there's no way you'd have gotten anybody to talk, even Gallagher. He'd have run to his friends and they would have disappeared. It was important we give them time to get settled in their organization."

"And kill more people?" Dane said. "Do more damage?"

"It wasn't like that. Royce, DeRocca and Gallagher were only just starting when they plugged in with the local Mafia. Their goals were always international, and they've finally found a sponsor who will take them to take them further."

"Some sort of benefactor?"

"Who he is, we don't know. Neither do we know where he is. There's more to this, now, than the three men who killed your father."

Dane sprang from the chair, his jaw clenched. He turned his back to the president, turned around again.

"You aren't going to convince me I should have told you sooner, Stephen. You had some growing to do. The best thing you could have done for yourself was take off on your own."

Dane's expression softened. He stepped over to the window overlooking the White House garden. The bright lights showed him some of the greenery, but shadows covered the rest.

"It's just like the old days," Dane said.

"Old spymasters never die," Cross said. "They just change offices."

"I have a file," Dane said. "From Gallagher's computer. I don't think it's the whole story, but I can prove they targeted US citizens, mob people."

"Uh-huh."

"But we aren't releasing anything to the press, are we?"

"Not if we can handle this in-house. Same as we handled your father's death. But we will establish the truth for those in the community who need to know. We will clear your father's name."

Dane turned from the window. "I don't know where to find Royce or DeRocca."

"Between you, Nina and Lukavina, that won't be the case for long."

"It's going to get bloody, sir."

"We wouldn't have it any other way, would we?"

Dane nodded.

"I still light a candle for you every day," Cross said.

"I think it helps."

The two men shook hands. Cross called an aid to escort Dane out. Dane left the room with his head spinning.

He didn't know what to make of the revelations, but, yeah, it was like the old days. Cross dumps a bunch of data and Dane acts.

And he planned to act in a big way.

Chapter Sixteen

Dane returned to the Watergate and paused at the entrance of the downstairs restaurant and adjoining bar. It wasn't the only bar in the hotel, but if Nina was going to give him a hard time about his sobriety order, she'd do it in the open where he could find her.

But she wasn't there. A hostess asked if he wanted a seat, but he excused himself. In the elevator, he watched the floor numbers above the door light up until the car stopped.

He found her at the table with a game of solitaire spread in front of her.

"I might get used to this not-drinking thing," she said.

"No, you won't."

She set down some more cards. He kept his eyes on her. He wasn't going to insult her by checking the wastebaskets.

"How did your meeting go?"

"Cross has known everything for a very long time."

She stopped halfway through a move and looked at him. "And he held it back because…?"

"I had some growing to do."

"He's probably right. You were certainly a mess when I met you."

Dane didn't smile. He knew Cross was probably right, and he hadn't argued, because the man had always been right. Dane had matured to understand that, then and now. But that didn't make it okay for him to hear. He had enough of an ego to want to argue just on principle.

"I bet you want a drink," Nina said.

Dane swallowed. His throat was dry. "You're right."

"Enough to break the fast?" She cracked half a grin.

"No."

She frowned and returned to her card game. Dane went into the bathroom, turned on the light, filled a glass with water and drank it down. He set it on the countertop. Hands on hips, he looked at his reflection. He saw a face tight with concentration. A man with a thousand thoughts racing through his mind.

"We'll talk to Len again tomorrow and see where he's at," he said.

"This one's kind of boring so far," she said.

He went over and rubbed her back. "The game?"

"Every time I think I have a match, I don't," she said. "I would probably have more fun with a vodka tonic or two."

Dane offered no reply. He moved behind Nina and began massaging her back.

"What's bothering you?" she said.

"What has been a mystery to me for so long," he said, "has been known for just as long to other people."

"How does that make you feel?"

"That's not the problem. The problem is that the answers are being handed to me on a plate."

"So?"

"It means that later, the obstacles will be ten times

harder."

She let out a frustrated grunt. "Like this stupid game."

He laughed. "When this is finished, I'll buy you a distillery."

"Two," she said, gathering the cards to reshuffle.

"Are you enjoying that game?"

"No," she said. "But it keeps the demons at bay."

Danes let her words filter through his mind.

He wanted to ask her what she meant but knew she wouldn't tell him. He left her alone to play cards and stretched out on the bed.

The next day Steve Dane, with Nina Talikova in tow, crossed the lobby seal of the Central Intelligence Agency and proceeded to the check-in desk. Lukavina came down to greet them and oversee the issuing of their green guest badges. The badges offered them very limited access, and they couldn't move about the building without an escort.

In the elevator, Nina said, "Back home we used to dream of entering this building."

"I bet," Lukavina said.

"We wanted to see how many bugs we could plant," Nina said.

"CIA headquarters has never been penetrated from the outside, and there have never been any listening devices discovered within these walls that our own people haven't put there."

"We wanted to change that," Nina said.

"Kids and their dreams," Dane quipped as the elevator doors opened. Nina gave him a glare he didn't see.

Lukavina led them into Figg's office, where the DCI rose from behind his desk.

"Mr. Dane, I apologize for the circumstances of our

meeting."

"All is forgiven." Dane crossed the office to shake the older man's hand. He introduced Nina. "I understand we're going to be able to work together on this."

"Not officially. Let's have a seat over there."

Figg sat everybody on leather couches with a glass coffee table between them, upon which were empty glasses, two pitchers of ice water and a plate of mini-carrots and celery. Figg told everybody to help themselves. Lukavina joined them last after collecting a tablet computer from the DCI's desk.

"I knew your father," Figg said.

"Really."

"Not very well. We passed each other in the hallway and worked on one project together."

"Uh-huh."

"We need to do whatever we can to expose this corruption."

"The president doesn't want to go public," Dane said.

"He told me the same thing. I meant figuratively. What's the Bible passage? 'Bring the darkness into light'?" Figg said with a slight chuckle.

"I'm not a religious scholar," Dane said.

"I used to be, but that was before I discovered this world isn't black and white and the answers are never easy."

Dane poured a glass of water and handed it to Nina, then poured another for himself. "I'm also not one for small talk."

Figg nodded. "Len has told me a lot about you. I'm a little sorry we never got to work together, and I haven't always supported your efforts, especially when they involved US interest, but we need each other now."

"Uh-huh."

"Len?"

Lukavina tapped the tablet's screen. He described his conversation with Detective Bishop and showed Dane and Nina pictures of Gino Moligano, his major lieutenants, as well as recent photos of Perry Royce and George DeRocca.

"George isn't aging well," Dane said.

"He's also in another line of work," Lukavina said. "We tracked him to a casino in Atlantic City. It's owned by one of Moligano's front companies. DeRocca is also in charge of a trucking company, and we think it's used as a cover to move contraband."

"How did you find him so fast?"

"He's using his real name, Steve."

"Probably no reason not to. What about Royce?"

"He's in Maryland, got a place on Chesapeake Beach. Lives alone, collects his pension, goes fishing now and then."

"And Moligano?"

"Nearby on a large estate with half a company of troops." Lukavina punched up the photo on the tablet, and Dane and Nina examined the aerial shot of the estate and the large amount of property.

Dane sat back and crossed his legs.

Figg said, "I don't think I need to advise you on any next steps, Mr. Dane. You probably already have some in mind."

Dane nodded. "Thank you both. But there's something missing."

"Which is?"

"President Cross spoke of a fourth man. Unknown. Some sort of benefactor that will take Royce and Moligano international."

"We're drawing a blank on that one so far," Lukavina

said. "But that kind of overseas connection certainly warrants our resources."

"I have another idea," Dane said. "Keep tabs on Royce and DeRocca. We'll start against Moligano and send the other two running to wherever their pal is."

"Plans rarely work out that way, Mr. Dane."

Dane admitted he understood that all too well.

"Unless you have a better idea, Mr. Figg, that's all I have to offer."

Len said, "I suggest we let Dane and Nina do their thing, sir. Dane's crazy enough to actually pull this off."

Figg nodded. He looked at Dane. "If you are caught or killed, this agency will deny everything."

"I expect nothing less," Dane said.

"Then blessings to you both," the DCI told him.

Dane left the CIA campus with a smile.

The time for vengeance had arrived.

Chapter Seventeen

"I have pictures for you, Mr. Royce," Andy Swindol said over the phone.

Perry Royce placed the long aluminum pool sweep on the concrete. "Of what?"

"Two people arrived today to see the director and Lukavina. I thought you might want their pictures. One of them used to work for us."

"Send them." Royce ended the call and tapped the screen to open Swindol's email when it arrived. The pictures showed a male and female at the security desk, a straight-on shot so their faces were perfectly visible.

The faces meant nothing.

Royce dialed Swindol.

"Yes, sir?"

"Who am I looking at?"

"The man is Steve Dane, who worked for Peter Cross when he was DCI. The woman is an FSB officer named Nina Talikova. They gave their contact address as the Watergate. I did a quick check and they're under their real names. Room 522."

Royce hung up without another word, his heart racing, and looked at the picture again. He should have recognized the man. He looked a lot like his father. Not a spitting image, but certainly enough features to know the two were related.

But the passing of time had dulled the memory. Now it came flooding back.

Steve Dane. Son of Richard.

The past had come back to haunt him. Now he knew who had killed Gallagher. They weren't facing the CIA. They were facing one man who had nothing to lose because he'd already lost so much. We should have killed the whole family in the very beginning. Leaving Dane alone to run around the world had been a monumental mistake.

His pulse still pounding, he dialed Hal Miller.

"I'm going to give you two names," Royce said. "They're at the Watergate. Room 522."

"Okay, go."

Royce spelled each name out and added, "Get back with Moligano and make sure he delivers on his promise to provide extra shooters. I don't want Dane and Talikova to survive the day."

"They won't."

Royce ended the call. He paused for dialing the next number. He had to update Cyrus Lassen, and Lassen would not appreciate the news once he heard the history of the Dane problem.

Royce dialed. Lassen answered. Royce spoke for several minutes and then stopped.

"Why did you let this man live after the helicopter crash, Perry?"

It was a fair question, but Royce had to admit he didn't know the answer. He provided the best answer he could, but now it made him sound like a weak sister who hadn't the fortitude to tie up all loose ends.

"Because he left," Royce said. "Quit the agency. Quit the country. All he cared about was himself. From all appearances, he stopped looking for answers once Cross told him to ignore the Russian he wanted to kill."

"Was he ever specifically looking for you?"

"No. None of his movements indicated that. He wanted the Russian. When Cross took that away, he left."

"And you also stopped watching him," Cyrus Lassen said. "Otherwise his reappearance wouldn't surprise you."

"Once we plugged in with your operations, Cyrus, he was kind of forgotten."

"You can't forget your enemies, Perry. You've compromised our whole operation."

"Miller is on the way to deal with him. And the woman."

"What about Carlton Figg and Len Lukavina?"

"They're not hard to find."

"By this point it's too late. Gallagher probably told them everything."

"We'll clean this up."

"Covering up the murders of several gangsters is a whole lot different than assassinating members of the intelligence community, Perry. Somebody will notice."

"What are you suggesting then?" Royce said. "The way I see it, the only other alternative is to admit defeat and take off running."

"Unless I have you killed."

"You could do that, but then I become another Gallagher. You won't be able to send your killers to me in time."

"Including Miller?"

"Especially Miller."

Lassen fell silent. Royce wondered how fast the gears were turning in his head. Royce added, "We've faced our share of setbacks. We surmounted all of them. There's no reason why we can't survive this."

Still nothing from Lassen. Royce stayed quiet.

Then: "You're going to need more than just Miller for these two, if what you say about their abilities is true."

All right! No surrender! Royce said, "We have Moligano and his people. They were made for this sort of thing."

"I expect the matter will be cleared by the end of the day."

"It will be."

Lassen said nothing for a moment. Perry Royce stood in the center of his den, the cell phone to his ear, the face of the phone wet from the sweat on the side of his head.

He knew the call wouldn't be pleasant but hadn't expected it to take the turn it had. At least he'd talked Lassen out of closing everything down. And treating him and DeRocca as loose ends.

"Anything else, Cyrus?"

Lassen remained quiet for another few seconds. Then: "Tell me this man's name again."

"Steve Dane. D-A-N-E."

"I thought so."

"What are you thinking?"

"Nothing that is any of your business, Perry. Stick to your tasks."

Lassen ended the call. Royce wiped off the front of his phone, then noticed his reflecting in the screen. He was frowning.

Did Dane mean something to Lassen as well?

At the presidential retreat in San Remo, Cyrus Lassen sat alone in the library. The walls were lined with books he'd never bothered to look at, and the intact spines suggested the books had never been read. He wasn't even sure El Presidente could actually read.

The windows were shut tight and the climate control throughout the mansion kept the building cool. Outside, more heat and humidity.

Lassen's face wore a tense expression as his mind finally connected the dots to who Steve Dane actually was.

The man who had killed his wife.

It had taken a long time for Lassen to collect the information on who had murdered the love of his life, the woman who was to share his empire, and when he discovered the man's identity, finally filed the name away for future reference. Lassen had decided that vengeance could wait. The dish wasn't cold enough. He needed San Remo free of the rebel problem, and set up the way he wanted, before he'd be able to concern himself with cutting the throat of the man who dropped a grenade on his wife.

But fate had other ideas. Lassen and Dane had been on a collision course, from separate ends, for a long time. He didn't need to find the man. Soon they'd find each other. Soon they'd meet face to face.

Lassen glanced to the left where a pair of French doors led to the balcony outside. He normally ate his lunch there and enjoyed the view, but ever since President Marco got the bright idea to dangle Lassen as bait for the rebels, he no longer followed the routine. And right now, he didn't feel remotely hungry.

The library door opened and the man in charge of Lassen's security force, the burly Sanchez, entered.

"Breach on the grounds, sir."

Lassen's attention snapped immediately to the present. He sat up a little on the couch. "Where?"

"South end."

"How many?"

"Cameras show three."

Lassen laughed quietly. "They took the bait."

"Yes, sir."

"Bring one in alive, Sanchez. It's been a couple of months since our last hunt."

"One alive, yes, sir."

Sanchez left the room.

Lassen sat back with a feeling of grim satisfaction. He wanted to lash out and kill somebody; the rebels had obliged a sacrifice.

Chapter Eighteen

The trip wire didn't set off a bomb.

Rico Gomez was a captain in the San Remo resistance force, which had taken the name The Sons of San Remo, Los Hijos de San Remo. Parts of the country secretly supported "the Sons" but it seemed an equal amount of the population actively worked against them. Moving through the urban areas required extreme caution.

There was always somebody looking to cash in on President Marco's offer for a reward leading to the capture of any rebel troops, especially commanding officers.

Approaching the presidential retreat, with its army security, required plenty of caution as well.

Captain Gomez held up his right hand as he and his two teammates crested a hill and looked down at the sprawling palace below them.

Gomez and his sergeant were lightly armed, carrying only automatic rifles, a pair of grenades, and navigation gear. They weren't planning for a long-term mission. Their mission to the retreat was hit-and-git, acting on information that might lead to the destruction of President

Marco's Gringo Dragon.

"There it is," Gomez said.

His sergeant, Benitez, inched closer to him for a better look. The heavy foliage around them obscured the view.

"I don't see any sign of the Gringo," Benitez said.

Rico Gomez checked his watch. Ten past noon. "He might be running late. Keep an eye on that balcony."

He gestured behind him for his other teammate to move forward. Corporal Jose Fuentes hauled with him a mortar tube and a backpack stuffed with shells. The only firearm the corporal carried was the autoloading pistol on his right hip.

Gomez told Fuentes to set up for the assault. Fuentes carefully placed the tube in position, extending the support legs, then carefully adjusting the range finder to the balcony on the side of the house where they expected Cyrus Lassen to appear for his afternoon lunch.

Benitez said, "A mistake? Is he not here today?"

Gomez wiped sweat from his forehead. "I hope not."

"Our sources—"

Gomez swiped a hand across his neck. Benitez stopped talking. Fuentes gave Gomez a thumbs up. The mortar was ready.

Gomez looked around, trying to pierce of forest coverage to spot a trap, any government soldiers in ambush.

Their sources in the Capitol city had reported that the Gringo Dragon, as Cyrus Lassen had been nicknamed by the Sons, had a habit of eating lunch on the balcony outside the retreat's library. But he wasn't stepping out.

Gomez, the brother of the rebel leader, scrambled with Benitez and Fuentes with a slapped-together assassination plan. If they had the opportunity to blow up the Gringo Dragon, and remove a major asset of President

Marco, the fight against the Marco regime might finally turn in their favor.

Cyrus Lassen, via contacts in the United States, supplied the San Remo army with guns and ammunition and other killing devices used against the rebels. Despite several raids on arms depots and blowing up trucks carrying weapons from the port region when they arrived, they hadn't been able to stop the flow of arms. The San Remo army had not been forced to resort to throwing rocks.

As more weapons arrived, more civilians were conscripted to fight the rebels. Gomez and his forces couldn't kill enough of them to turn the tide.

Kill Lassen and maybe they'd have a chance at victory. And Rico Gomez and his brother Roberto certainly wouldn't mind a small taste of revenge. Lassen would be the appetizer; Diego Marco himself the main course.

Lassen provided money and support to the Marco regime. Without him, Marco would lose his access of arms and a valuable contact with the criminal underworld outside San Remo.

The three men remained silent. Noises from the compound below did not reach them. Leaves rustled with shorts bursts of breeze that did nothing to cool the sweating that soaked their uniforms.

Gomez checked his watch. One hour past the time the informers had said Lassen usually went outside and no servants emerged to serve the meal. The table was there, sans cloth or setting. For some reason, Lassen was breaking the routine. Gomez told Fuentes to pack up the mortar. They were going back to camp. They'd picked the wrong day. Perhaps they'd try again another time.

They started up the slope to the crest of the hill once again, then started down, guiding around some fallen logs and tree debris. The debris steered them well off the course they'd followed up the hill, and as Gomez looked for a way to get them back on track, Fuentes hit the ground hard.

Gomez ran to him while Benitez shouldered his automatic rifle to scan for targets.

"I hit something," Fuentes said.

Gomez examined the ground near Fuentes' ankles, something twinkling in the sun below the greenery. He brushed the debris aside and picked up part of a steel wire.

"A trip wire but nothing exploded."

"Captain," Benitez said. He pointed at a tree.

Gomez looked where the sergeant pointed. The camera hidden under a branch was clearly focused on them.

"A sensor to activate the camera," Gomez said. He helped Fuentes to his feet. "They see us and they know where to find us. Come on!"

The rebel troops ignored stealth and stomped through the forest. A covert escape had become a run for their lives.

The whipping rotor blades of a chopper sounded in the distance, growing in volume.

Gomez wasn't sure they'd be able to run fast enough to beat the devils chasing them.

Hal Miller called Gino Moligano with good news.

"We found the two people we're looking for and need the backup you promised."

"You'll have them. Where are you?"

Miller told the big boss where the extra guys should meet him and hung up.

Miller presently arrived at the Watergate and parked at the curb along New Hampshire Avenue facing the Potomac. He left the car and began scouting the property, his eyes never far from the outside of the fifth floor. Room 522 sat near the opening of the crescent-shaped building near the river. On the sixth floor was an observation deck, above which a floor of conference rooms and more guest rooms stretched upward into the sky. The deck held his attention.

He made a mental list of needed equipment and returned to his car, traveling a few blocks to a coffee shop, where he ordered a Coca-Cola and selected a table against the wall.

When Moligano's gun monkeys arrived, Miller waved them over. They sat down and introduced themselves, but Miller didn't bother to remember their names. They were Gun Monkey One and Gun Monkey Two. Cannon fodder in case Steve Dane and Nina Talikova managed to fire off a few rounds. Miller wasn't an idiot. He had learned of their reputation as quick shooters, and they hadn't survived by being stupid.

He was better than them, though. He proved it with every kill.

Inwardly, he grumbled at Gino Moligano. He'd asked for back-up, and that certainly implied more than two shooters. The gangster was playing games. Miller decided not to give the man the satisfaction of a complaint. Two shooters would have to do. It was better than going after Dane and Talikova on his own.

After a trip to a sporting goods store, where Miller acquired the items on his list, they started preparing for the night strike.

Chapter Nineteen

Captain Rico Gomez watched three soldiers descend from the chopper on ropes. As the trio landed on the forest floor, he and Benitez, concealed behind large leaves several meters apart to try for a crossfire, set their sights and opened fire.

The rebels issued any weapons they could get their hands on, and in the case of Gomez and Sergeant Benitez, they used American M-16A1 rifles originally issued in the '80s. They never asked how the various arms dealers they contracted with acquired the weapons; they only asked that they work, and the rifles the two men fired worked well, spitting 5.56mm lead at the descending chopper troopers without mercy.

The barrage of hot lead dropped two of the troopers before they disengaged their rappelling lines. The third dropped and rolled free of his harness, diving into the brush. Gomez aimed where he thought the solider went, fired a burst, but his salvo only stitched through the foliage without smacking flesh.

"One more!" Benitez yelled.

Gomez lifted his muzzle and tried to shoot the last trooper sliding down the nylon rope, but each shot missed. He fired at the chopper, rounds bouncing off the belly of the machine before the pilot turned and flew away, the third and final soldier quickly vanishing into the brush like his partner.

Gomez and Benitez reloaded and started running, Fuentes joining them. He'd ditched the heavy mortar. They had no use for the tube now. The only thing that mattered at this moment was survival and escape. Fuentes clutched his pistol; the man's young face dripped sweat.

Gomez slapped at his neck as he ran, as his own sweat trickled down, and the three huffed as they dodged natural obstacles in the effort to put major distance between them and the two hunters.

Branches and leaves slapped at his face as they ran, but he had no idea which direction they were going. His compass was stowed. They were, for sure, off the path they'd followed earlier. They needed to get away from the men chasing them, and then plot their way back to camp.

First, survival.

Fuentes screamed.

Gomez turned as the young man's body went thud at the bottom of a pit, the covering fodder mostly still over the deep hole, a spot Gomez and Benitez had barely missed in their headlong rush.

Gomez looked. Fuentes lay at the bottom, his upper body and lower legs impaled on sharp steel spikes, his face frozen in a contortion of agony, eyes still open.

Benitez cursed.

"Run," Gomez said.

The sprint began anew.

Sanchez heard the scream and maintained his running pace.

He and his backup gunner skirted the pit with the dead rebel at the bottom and continued after the other two, Sanchez stopping long enough to trigger a burst from his submachine gun that ripped through the vegetation ahead. His partner pitched a grenade that landed near one of the rebels, anther scream splitting the air as the man died and bits of him landed across the jungle floor.

One left.

Sanchez and the second gunner zeroed on the man's back. They knew the area; the rebel didn't. Sanchez's boots landed surely on the ground; the obstacles known to him; the noise from stomping leaves and branches as he ran not a concern. He ducked and dodged the lower branches, jumped the fallen logs and branches.

The last rebel ran well, and Sanchez hustled to speed up, but he didn't want to tire himself. The rebel might get tired very quickly at the rate he was running.

When they finally started to gain on the lone man, the second gunner broke right, and Sanchez knew his plan. He'd cut around in a circle to intercept the rebel from either the side or front. It was a maneuver they'd perfected over several hunts like this.

Sanchez knew this pursuit didn't qualify as the "hunt" Lassen had in mind. Those were much better. Sanchez liked it when the prey had the chance to fight back.

The rebel ahead tried to jump over a moss-covered tree trunk that lay on its side. He almost made it, landing short and colliding with the trunk instead. He scrambled over the side, tossing his rifle over first, and as Sanchez finally found himself in shooting range the rebels legs vanished over the side.

Sanchez triggered a salvo, stitching the tree. A grenade sailed over the top of the log and Sanchez dropped and rolled left. The grenade went off behind him, bits of shrapnel tearing at the vegetation around him, but causing no harm to him.

Another salvo in front of the trunk kicking up dirt. Sanchez needed the man pinned. He might not see the other gunner moving up alongside.

Sanchez continued left, working through the vegetation and around the fallen log. The ground sloped a little, but then started up again, and he inched along as the rebel continued firing short bursts at targets with which he had no visual contact.

We need him alive! Sanchez reminded himself. It would be so easy to shoot the rebel and let his body rot with the other two.

Sanchez finally moved close enough to burst through the leaves and jam the hot muzzle of his weapon the rebel's neck. He shouted for the man not to move.

At the same moment, Sanchez's partner emerged from cover, swinging his muzzle on the rebel as well.

The rebel, looking over his right shoulder at Sanchez with defiance, dropped his rifle and raised his hands.

Sanchez enjoyed a laugh.

Time for war.

Urban combat, specifically.

Dane snapped back the slide on the stainless steel Detonics Scoremaster .45 and upped the safety. He popped the gun into his shoulder harness. He and Nina both wore black head to toe. She sat on the bed and gave the laces on her boots one extra tug before tying the knots.

Dane moved a heavy case out of the closet and set it on the bed. The case, and the lethal items inside, had been supplied by Dane's pal Devlin Stone, an arms dealer and a smuggler who had worked with Dane in his mercenary days. Lifting the lid, he started laying out loaded magazines and a pair of beat-up Uzi submachine guns. Nina selected one and worked the shoulder strap so it positioned the weapon under her right arm. She drew on a coat that covered the Uzi. Dane pulled on his own short topcoat and filled the pockets with spare magazines. Nina took the remaining mags. Finally, they helped themselves to a trio of hand grenades, which filled any remaining pocket space.

Dane found a folding Buck knife and added that to a pocket.

The last items Dane took from the case were six-inch tubes, black, also scuffed. Silencers. He handed one to Nina.

"Ready?" he said.

"Let's have an old-fashioned hammer party," she said.

It was time to meet Gino Moligano, the first step in the plan to wipe out Perry Royce and his crew of killers.

Chapter Twenty

Room 522 sat in darkness; the drapes closed.

Two taps on the door.

Outside, slightly visible through the drapes, the end of a rope appeared. Presently Hal Miller lowered himself from the upper observation deck to the balcony outside 522, his feet touching the top of the railing. He jumped onto the patio, dropped behind a chair and pulled a silenced pistol.

Two more knocks on the door.

Miller used a glass cutter on the patio door. The blade made a light screech as he made a circle in the glass near the lock. Sliding his free hand in, he opened the sliding glass door and stepped into the empty room.

Another knock.

Miller turned on a light and made his way to the door. "It's me," he called, and unlocked the deadbolt and chain. Gun Monkey One and Two stood in the hallway. He stepped back for them to enter.

"Now what?" said Monkey One.

Miller took out his phone. "If they aren't here, I have a feeling I know where they'll be." He dialed quickly.

Dane stopped the car just off the shoulder on Riverview Road. He and Nina hopped out and crossed the pavement to a line of trees where the ground sloped into a ditch. They dropped into the ditch and leaned against the opposite rise. Across an open field, following a long access road, sat Moligano's mansion. Lights burned inside the house.

It wasn't a multi-story home, but instead single level and stretched out over the center of the surrounding grassy field. Trees lined the edge of the property and provided cover from the road.

Starting on the left side of the mansion was an opening for a large garage; the main living spaces continued on to the right of the garage.

Nina put a set of night-vision binoculars to her eyes. Dane scanned the darkness. The grass and the dirt below were dry, and he swiped away a bug that flew across his face. He had never liked grass, going back to hot summer days at home when it stuck to his skin during football and smelled funny when he was face down in the prickly green stuff after a tackle.

"I don't see any troops," she said.

"They're out there. With dogs, more than likely."

"Do we want to risk a battle here?"

"We're isolated enough."

"But close enough that the neighbors will report the gunfire."

"That's why we have silencers."

"Do they?"

"We're doing this, Nina."

She said nothing more and continued to look through the binoculars. "Wait. There they are. Doorway near the garage. No dogs. Two men, splitting up. They're going in different directions for a walk around the property."

Dane checked his watch and made a note of the time. "Let's watch what they do."

They passed the night-vision binoculars back and forth, noting the movements of the two troopers. Neither guard carried automatic weapons, only sidearms. They didn't go more than fifty yards from the house, counting on flash-lights to illuminate the areas before them. After thirty min-utes they went back through the door.

Dane and Nina waited another half hour until the troops exited the house once again for another round.

"Thirty-minute intervals," Dane said, checking his watch again. The troops made their usual rounds and went back inside.

"Now," Dane said. He bolted from the ditch, jamming the stock of the Uzi into his shoulder. His boots pounded on the grass and he heard Nina running behind him, her breathing faster than his. They blended into the dark, the mansion looming ahead. Within fifteen yards of the house, bright lights flashed to life, lighting up a twenty-yard radi-us. An alarm joined the lights.

Dane and Nina cut left, heading for the door near the garage. As they approached, the door opened and two men with drawn pistols emerged. Dane opened fire. The Uzi bucked against his shoulder, the clicking of the action mechanism making more noise than the phuts coming from the silenced snout. Nina stopped beside him and loosed her own salvo. The two gunners screamed as the rounds split them open, their bodies tumbling to the ground in a tangle.

Dane and Nina moved onto the polished concrete floor of a side room connected to the main garage full of antique and exotic cars parked on either side. They stopped beside a yellow Lamborghini with tinted windows. Between them and a door that presumably led into the main house was a wide-open space of more polished concrete. The door opened and another pair of gunmen came out, splitting up, shouting orders for them to surrender.

"They're not going to shoot at us with the cars here," Dane said.

"What do you suggest?"

Dane slung the Uzi and plucked a grenade from his belt. "I hate to do this," he said, yanking the pin and rolling the grenade across the floor. It stopped near the front end of a Model T. He pulled Nina further behind the yellow Lambo. The explosion rocked the walls and shook the floor and sent a fireball into the ceiling, peppering the surrounding vehicles with debris. One gunman let out a scream.

"Go!"

Dane charged ahead through the growing gray smoke, Nina behind him. He sprayed rounds at the spot where he thought the gunmen were hiding. One tumbled out of the smoke into the open, coughing; Nina zipped him stomach to chest with a quick burst. They reached the opposite door as the fire alarm began to blare. Dane's lungs strained in the heat and smoke. He and Nina crashed through the doorway and into the house, breathing in the untainted air.

A circular room with a checkered tile floor, the front door to their left. They met a gunman halfway. He was out of breath, clutching a pistol. Dane shot him in the chest. The man's momentum carried him forward, and he fell at their feet. Stepping over him, Dane and Nina continued their advance, reloading as they reached a guest room. Properly made bed, Renaissance paintings on the wall. Dane entered and scanned with his eyes and weapon. Empty. They moved to another door. Somebody started yelling from the other side.

Chapter Twenty-One

It had been a quiet night until the explosion rocked the garage.

Gino Moligano sat in the large family room, behind a table, working on a puzzle. The picture forming showed a horse in the middle of a field of green not unlike the field that surrounded his home, though the puzzle included a touch of fog they hardly ever saw. Two of his bodyguards sat on a nearby couch reading and watching ESPN. They and the others patrolled the property in shifts, as usual, and as Moligano fitted one piece to another and found where they belonged in the big picture, he had expected another quiet night.

Then the house shook as something went boom.

The bodyguards jumped from the couch, drawing weapons. Moligano stepped back from the table, crossed to a desk and took out his own pistol. As he checked the load, one of the bodyguards left the room. The other said, "If that came from the garage—"

"Where else?"

The fire alarm began blaring.

"We stand and fight right here," the capo said.

"Yes, sir."

Moligano's cell phone rang. "What?"

Miller identified himself and explained that the people they were looking for weren't in the hotel and might be on their way to his place.

"I oughta give you a prize or something," Moligano said, a little louder than he intended. "They're here and we're outgunned!" He threw the phone down.

Moligano tipped over the table, the half-completed puzzle and stray pieces crashing to the floor. He helped his bodyguard move the couch to block the door.

They took cover behind the overturned table. The capo's heart pounded in his chest. His eyes never left the door. This wasn't his first fight, and he had no intention of its being his last.

Dane and Nina approached the door, Dane dropping to his stomach and crawling. Nina shouldered her Uzi as he readied another grenade. He turned the doorknob and gave it a pull. Gunfire cracked from the opposite side, punching through the wood, the bullets whizzing by, the wooden shards flying in all directions. Nina fired a burst, tearing more holes in the door, and Dane pitched the grenade through the gap. It detonated with a crash that blew the door off the hinges. It fell like a tree. Somebody screamed.

Through the doorway—right into the couch. Dane dropped behind it, Nina landing beside him. Smoke hovered below the ceiling as a section of carpet burned. Somebody shot from behind an overturned table. Dane returned fire and watched a bodyguard jerk with the impact of the burst. As he fell, a second man, Moligano, bolted across the room, using furniture for cover as he made for the windows. Dane fired and missed. The smoke obscured his aim and covered the target well. Glass crashed as Moligano appeared again, throwing a heavy end table through the window. Dane raised the Uzi. Moligano fired two rounds over his shoulder, driving Dane and Nina down as he leaped into the night.

Nina moved around the side of the couch and fired through what remained of the window, stitching a pattern through the wall, trying to hit the fleeing capo. Dane vaulted over the couch and ran through the smoke. She called after him as she reloaded once again. Dane dived through the window and landed hard on the cold grass outside. As he gained his feet, he brought up his weapon. Moligano, caught in the blaze of the security lights, huffed as he ran into the darkness.

The fire alarm echoed in the night—or were sirens screeching in the distance? Dane could not hear. The gunfire and grenade blasts had left his ears ringing.

He and Nina entered the splash of security light as Moligano disappeared into the night. Dane thought he saw the man turn and raise his gun. Dane and Nina dropped and rolled as the shots cracked above them. Dane stopped on his stomach and let a long burst go. Moligano yelled. Dane fired again. The yelling stopped.

Dane ran to the body, kicking the man's gun away and dragging him back into the pool of light. Moligano let out a moan, blood bubbling out of his mouth, his chest and legs opened by the salvo of 9-millimeter stingers. Then his eyes froze open and he breathed no more.

Dane and Nina ran breathlessly across the field, back toward the road. Sirens were unmistakable now. They had minutes—maybe less—to escape. Someone's spotting them at a scene of such carnage was the last thing they needed.

At the car, Dane opened the trunk and they stripped off their weapons and gear. Nina jumped behind the wheel and started the engine. Dane slammed the trunk.

And the headlights of an onrushing car lit him up.

Dane moved quickly around the passenger side. The other car sped by, then the brake lights flared, and the tires screeched. Somebody leaned out the back window and raised his right arm. Dane yelled for Nina to get down as a flame flashed from the man's gun. Dane dived into the car. Nina shifted into reverse and powered backward, leaving a cloud of tire smoke behind. She grabbed the handbrake and yanked up hard. The tires squealed again as she wrenched the wheel and spun the car 180 degrees. She released the brake and stomped on the gas. The car lurched forward, the engine letting out a strangled roar.

"Don't give me too many bumps," Dane said as he crawled from the front seat to the back. As the car surged ahead, rocking to and fro as Nina took turns too sharply, Dane found the rear seat's release cable and pulled. A section of the rear backrest folded his way, and he felt around in the trunk for their weapons. His hands grasped his shoulder harness, and he grabbed the .45. Flashes of light from streetlamps highlighted the bright stainless steel of his Detonics Scoremaster.

"They're still with us and gaining fast," Nina said.

The road straightened. Dane raised his head enough to see the pursuing car but couldn't make out the driver's face or the number of occupants.

Who was in that car?

Chapter Twenty-Two

"Get closer!" said Gun Monkey Two from the back seat.

Hal Miller, his foot mashing the gas pedal to the floor, was giving the engine all it had now that the road had straightened and their target wasn't pulling away. Cold air filled the car as Monkey Two rolled down the window.

Gun Monkey One, in the passenger seat next to Miller, readied his own pistol.

Miller had seen the flames from Moligano's house as they'd approached. The capo was a goner. What mattered now was taking out the two troublemakers.

They were roaches in a kitchen, as far as Miller was concerned.

Dane powered down the back-passenger window, and the cold chill bit hard.

"Turn coming!" Nina shouted.

Dane leaned out with the .45 in his left hand as the back-seat passenger from the chase car popped out with his own weapon. The wind slammed hard into Dane's back and made it hard to steady his aim. He didn't bother aiming at the gunman. He fired twice into the windshield, the glass sprouting spider web cracks, then twice into the hood. His one shot at the front tire missed and whined off into the night.

The passenger slammed a hand to his left shoulder, the driver hitting the brakes to drop back. The gunman in back fired, but his shots came nowhere near Dane.

"Steve!"

Dane dropped back inside as Nina took a sharp left. Only another mile or two before they could get lost in downtown traffic.

"Where to?" she said.

"We need to get to Len," Dane said, digging for his phone. "Now that we've hit them, he'll be a target."

Nina kept driving as Dane dialed.

Hal Miller braked hard and pulled off the road into a turnout.

Gun Monkey One, beside him, clutched his bloody shoulder and moaned, rocking his body from side to side. His shirt was soaked, the .45 slug having punched through his shoulder to embed itself in the back seat. Gun Monkey Two tore a piece from his own shirt and made Monkey One stop long enough to tie a crude tourniquet. Monkey One still groaned.

Maybe they weren't so dumb after all.

Miller took out his phone and started to dial.

"Anybody got morphine?" Monkey One said.

"I can hit you over the head and knock you out," said Monkey Two.

"Okay, why not?"

Monkey Two reversed his grip on his automatic and bashed Monkey One with the butt. The blow glanced off, and Monkey One screamed. Monkey Two hit him again.

Monkey One screamed.

"You hit like a girl!"

Monkey Two said, "Quit moving," and brought the butt down one more time. This time Monkey One slumped against the door and stopped moving. Monkey Two quickly felt for a pulse in his compatriot's neck.

"Well, I didn't kill him," he said.

Miller shook his head and withdrew his previous assessment.

The other line picked up.

"Yes?"

"Moligano's dead and they're heading your way."

"We're ready."

Dane put away his phone.

"No answer?" Nina said.

"No answer," he said, "and that's bad."

Nina made a left turn. "We can be there in twenty minutes."

Dane looked behind them. Why hadn't the other car stayed with them? A knot of tension lodged in his stomach. He didn't like how this was playing out so far.

Nina jerked the car to a stop in front of Lukavina's house.

The spotlight hit them as soon as they left the vehicle.

The light blazed from an open window. They dived and rolled as pistol fire whined overhead. Dane fired a three-round burst. Glass shattered and the light went out.

Nina jumped up and raced forward. She kicked open the door, entered and rolled left. Dane, on her heels, swept the Uzi right to left.

They were in the front room, with couches, chairs and a piano. Hallway straight ahead. A gunman near the piano rose with a pistol; Dane pinned him to the wall with another burst. The gunman fell and got tangled in some curtains, leaving a trail of red as he hit the ground.

Another gunman fired twice from a doorway along the hall. Dane fired back only to miss and tear chunks out of the wall.

The gunman emerged again, this time to fling a smoke grenade their way. The living room filled with smoke. It stung Dane's eyes and went up his nose. He coughed, dropping low.

Dane ran forward into the smoke only to collide with the hallway gunner. He might as well have tried plowing through a brick wall. He saw enough of the man to know he was not only huge but wore a gas mask. The collision had sent the man's gun flying, but he was still ready for a fight.

He slammed Dane against the wall. Dane exhaled sharply. The gunner tried to wrench the Uzi from Dane's grasp, but Dane held tight, pulling the gunman closer. He raised a knee but missed the thug's privates. The gunman kept one hand on the Uzi and grabbed a fistful of Dane's shirt with the other. He kicked one of Dane's legs out from under him and shoved Dane to the floor, landing on top. Then his beefy hands grabbed Dane around the neck. He squeezed hard. Dane choked, his airway cut off as he tried to inflate his lungs, his eyes still hot and wet from the smoke. He tried to buck off his attacker, but he might as well have been trying to move a ton of marble.

He heard Nina's Uzi crackle from somewhere in the house.

The open front door and the breeze from outside began clearing some of the smoke. Through the plastic front of the gas mask, Dane watched the gunman's unblinking eyes go wide as he squeezed harder.

Chapter Twenty-Three

Dane had no more options. He let go of the Uzi and grasped the killer's gas mask, yanking it aside, exposing one eye and obscuring the other.

The remaining smoke hit the gunman hard. That one big eye took the brunt of it and he recoiled. He tried to adjust the mask, but Dane pressed the index and middle finger of his right hand together, then blasted a two-finger strike into the gunman's throat.

The gunman let out a squeal and rolled away. Dane rolled to his knees, gasping for air. The gunman tossed the mask and started to charge again.

The Buck knife snapped open in Dane's hand. He met the gunman halfway, plunging the knife into him. Dane stabbed him again and again, leaving the thug a dead weight against him. He shoved the gunman away, wiped the bloody knife on the man's pants, stowed it and picked up the Uzi.

Only residual smoke from the grenade hung in the air. Dane leaned against the wall for a moment. The fight had taken almost everything out of him.

An engine roared and something crashed outside.

"Nina!"

A gun blast roared somewhere.

"Nina!"

No answer.

Nina shut her eyes and clamped her free left hand over her nose and mouth as the room filled with smoke. The last thing she saw before the smoke engulfed the room was the doorway to the kitchen—straight ahead, past the piano and corner dining table.

She ran that way, catching a foot on the leg of a dining chair. She fell face first onto the carpet. Somebody screamed from the kitchen. Nina jumped up and ran through the doorway.

A fourth gunman hauled a middle-aged woman from the laundry room adjacent to the kitchen. Mrs. Lukavina. Nina realized she didn't know the woman's name. The man kept the woman close, but then she twisted out of his grip and for a split-second Nina had a kill shot. But as she tightened on the Uzi's trigger, the gunman pulled the woman to him again. Nina raised the muzzle at the last instant and fired her blast into the ceiling.

Plaster rained down on Nina as the gunman hauled Mrs. Lukavina across the tiled floor to a patio door.

The gunman fired at Nina, missed and opened the door, dragging the woman outside. Nina started to follow but the gunman fired into the house, Nina hitting the floor as the stingers shredded the cupboard and refrigerator.

Nina jumped up and ran outside in time to see the thug carry Mrs. Lukavina around the corner.

Nina stopped and peeked around the corner. A shot from the gunman hit the outer wall and spit bits of shrapnel into

Nina's face. She yelled, ducking back. A doorway to the garage was midway down the walkway. The door opened with a squeak. She turned the corner and advanced.

An engine started.

Nina ran.

As she cleared the doorway, she watched a black SUV plow backward through the garage door, whole pieces clinging to the back of the SUV.

Nina fired, flame licking from the Uzi's muzzle. The SUV sank forward on two flat front tires, half out of the garage. Nina's next blast shattered the windscreen and took off part of the gunman's head. The SUV idled in reverse, the steel rims of the front wheels screeching on the concrete.

Nina ran to the driver's side, opening the door. She reached across the dead gunman, threw the vehicle into Park, and looked at the frightened lady on the floor of the passenger side.

She pointed over Nina's shoulder.

"Look out!"

Nina waited for bullets to hit her as she spun around.

"It's me!" Dane shouted, holding up his Uzi. Len Lukavina, tearing remnants of rope from his wrists, followed him. His wife bolted from the car and into her husband's arms.

Dane drove this time, scenery flashing by, Nina beside him on the passenger side and the Lukavinas in the back seat.

"What happened, Steve?" Len said.

"We hit Moligano," Dane said, adding a brief description of the fight.

Lukavina's wife grabbed her husband's arm with both hands and squeezed tightly. "The girls!"

"Are they local?" Dane said.

"California and Arizona," Len replied, his wife loosening her grip.

"Better call them just in case."

"There's a local safe house we can use for now," Len said.

"Just tell me how to get there."

At the safe house, Dane and Nina sat with steaming mugs of tea on a couch with a coffee table in front of them. The table was as bare and antiseptic as the rest of the house, which resembled a model home in a real estate development rather than any living space.

Mrs. Lukavina sat away from them while her husband paced near the dining table and spoke to DCI Figg over the secured landline. Both still wore their pajamas.

Dane looked at Nina. "I forgot to ask if you were okay."

"No holes I wasn't already born with," she said, swallowing some tea.

Dane grinned but straightened his face when he caught Mrs. Lukavina's death stare.

Her name was Angie and this was only the second time in his life that Dane had seen her. The first was at Bethesda, where her husband had been treated after nearly burning to death.

He didn't blame her for being angry.

Lukavina put down the phone and found another chair, which he pulled close to the coffee table. "We're gonna have some explaining to do for the cops, but the agency will cover it."

"What about you two?" Dane said.

"We'll hang here till further notice, probably another forty-eight hours or so."

Angie Lukavina started to protest, but Len held up a hand. "We'll have personal items brought here by a security team, hon, don't worry."

"This is insane," she said.

"I know."

Lukavina turned to Dane. The two friends didn't say anything for a few moments. Dane wondered if Len wanted to help finish the mission. If their places had been reversed, Dane knew he'd ask to tag along. Len had as much personal investment in the outcome as Dane had. But as much as he might want his pal fighting beside him, he knew, and suspected that Lukavina knew as well, that he was more valuable at headquarters.

And then there was Angie in the equation. She was pissed now; she'd be furious if he even brought up the idea as a hypothetical question.

"And now I need to know about you two," Lukavina finally said.

"Time to deal with Royce," Dane said.

Chapter Twenty-Four

Captain Rico Gomez woke up on a bed.

His uniform had been stripped off, but new clothes had been draped on a chair on the other side of the room.

Rico looked around with a frown. His last memory was of having a hot gun barrel jabbed into his neck, and now he was in a small bedroom, with a barred window, plush carpeting and wallpaper that didn't look gaudy. There was a bathroom, too, and he wandered in to splash water on his face and then he checked the clothes.

They fit well, and his combat boots had been shined and placed on the floor next to the chair. Within the right boot, Rico Gomez found his dog tags. Name, blood type, religion. He put the chain around his neck.

The chair sat in front of a corner desk and he quickly searched the drawers for any stray items that might make a close-quarter weapon, but every drawer was empty.

He sat on the bed and waited. Sun streaming through the window told him it was probably the day after his capture. But this was no prison cell. Or was it? He left the bed and tried the doorknob. Locked. He nodded. A cell, yes. But a strange one indeed. He sat on the bed again and waited some more.

The lock clicked and the door opened and the swarthy man who had captured him stood there. The man said, "Follow me."

Rico didn't ask any questions. He followed the burly man, who had brought a guard with him. The guard carried an automatic rifle. Rico didn't try to grab it. He had no idea where in the presidential retreat he was or where he might find an exit. Better to wait and see what happened.

They walked down a long hallway.

If they knew who he was, Rico figured the executioners might hold back a while.

Presently Rico was taken through the library and out a pair of French doors to a balcony where Cyrus Lassen, the Gringo Dragon, wearing a white suit, sat at a table with two place setting.

"Welcome, Captain, I hope you enjoy this close-up look at the balcony you wanted to blow up."

Rico looked around as the burly man and guard stepped away.

"What's the meaning of this?" Rico said. "What games are you playing?"

"You're going to need your energy, Captain, please sit and eat."

"I'm not eating anything you serve."

"Then you'll only die hungry."

"Explain."

Lassen chuckled. He sipped a glass of ice water with a slice of lemon in the ice.

"You need your strength, Captain. After lunch, you will be given a head start, and then my men will come after you. This is the deal. If you survive the jungle around my home and the traps I'm sure you rebels are familiar with, then you're free to go."

"And if I don't?"

"We'll leave your body to rot out there. You'll have plenty of company, Captain, so don't worry about dying alone."

Rico Gomez blinked.

"Nobody has ever escaped my hunters. There are a lot of bones out there."

Gomez refused to respond. He'd heard rumors of the "Dragon Hunt" as they had become known, but very few people believed the stories were true. Brutal executions, yes. Labor camps, sure. Letting a prisoner free if he survived a gauntlet? That was the stuff of fiction.

But now he knew the rumors were true.

"Are you going to eat something?" Lassen said.

"I suppose I better."

Rico sat. Lassen smiled. Despite the heat of the day, Captain Rico Gomez felt a chill flash up his back.

Waves crashing on the beach usually calmed Perry Royce, but not tonight. An anxiety like he'd never known before filled him. Moligano was already gone. Dane was on the warpath and not letting anything stand in his way.

He'd called Lassen twice without reaching him which was infuriating. What was the son of a bitch doing in his tropical paradise while the rest of them were getting killed off?

When he finally spoke with Cyrus and explained the situation, Lassen told him it was best if Perry left the area. Try the estate in Europe. Dane won't find you there, Lassen said. Lassen added that he had a plan to lure Dane to San Remo, and then they'd be able to clear their obstacles and continue "the plan".

"What about DeRocca?" Royce said.

"Every fisherman needs bait, Perry."

"We aren't going to have much of an organization if we kill our own people, Cyrus."

"With only the two of us, there will be less money to spread around."

Royce had felt two emotions at once. Anger again, because another friend had a target on his back, and agreement with the plan, because Dane was insane. He told Lassen to send a chopper and then alerted DeRocca to the issue and told him to stand ready.

Because once Royce slipped from Dane's grasp, the son of Richard Dane would scorch the earth looking for him.

Of that Perry Royce had no doubt.

The ocean stretched ahead of him to infinity, the dark sky making the normally blue water look black, and from the patio where he stood it looked like an abyss inviting him to his death. There was still a chance for escape, though, if the chopper arrived in time. He'd built a wooden dock a long time ago for his own boat, and it sat anchored on the left side, but escaping by boat wasn't a good option. Too many things could happen on the water. It was also too slow. Even if he escaped before Dane's arrival, Dane could muster a search team and end Royce's plans before the sun rose again.

He checked his watch and looked upward into the sky. No sign of the chopper. He'd at least see the lights. The waves would drown out the sound of the rotor blades until the chopper came close.

A voice behind him. "Mr. Royce."

He turned. The tip of his cane scraped the patio. Hal Miller approached, his boots sinking into the soft sand as he walked. "We're all set."

Royce nodded. Miller and his two gun monkeys had arrived minutes before. One wasn't in very good shape, it seemed, but he could still shoot, and the pistol on Royce's hip was another gun on their side. Miller had said Dane had only the Talikova woman with him.

"Good."

Royce followed Miller back inside. They'd turned off the lights and navigated the interior via flashlight. It was the one time Royce regretted having so much glass on the lower floor. He'd wanted to be able to see the ocean from any room on the first floor, a choice that might prove fatal.

The gun monkeys had placed a couch before the front window as a barricade. On their knees behind it, they held weapons ready. Miller moved upstairs to another window, a pair of binoculars in hand, to get the high view. Royce took out his pistol and found a chair to crouch behind, his cane to one side. He checked his watch. Where was that damn chopper?

Chapter Twenty-Five

Dane and Nina left their car on the side of Bayview Road and stomped through the forest. The splashing waves guided them to the shore. When they reached the edge where sand met foliage, they stopped. Royce's home sat about twenty-five meters to their left.

"Still have some grenades?" Dane said.

"All of them."

"Let's go."

They ran low across the sand, grunting with effort from the lack of traction, having to raise their feet higher than normal to keep moving, Dane almost losing his balance as they neared the structure. The darkened house filled Dane with a sense of foreboding. Had Royce already fled? Only one way to find out.

He shouldered the Uzi and fired a string of silenced shots into a side window. The glass dropped from the frame, the crash of pieces loud despite the competing ocean. Nina tossed one grenade and then the other. The explosives sailed through the opening, and somebody let out a panicked scream. Both explosions shook the ground. Dane led the way with Nina behind him, the Uzi up and his eyes scanning for targets. He leaped through the opening and pivoted left. Two men near a couch. The Uzi bucked. One man dropped. The other fired once before Dane stitched him stomach to chest.

"Steve!"

A lone figure ran for the rear doors. He fired over his shoulder, the bullet slicing the air beside Dane's head. Dane and Nina lined up and fired, the patio doors shattering, the figure ducking through unscathed. The man limped into the night.

"The stairs!" Nina shouted.

Dane pivoted again. Another man slid down the banister and hit the ground in a roll, coming up to open fire as Dane and Nina scrambled for cover. Nina returned fire as Dane changed magazines.

"Take him!" he said, cutting across Nina's line of fire. More shooting behind him as he cleared the shattered doors and charged after the man running along the beach.

Hal Miller slithered forward across the tile to the carpet, stopping beside the wreckage of Royce's furniture. One had gone; one remained. He sensed movement and fired a shot. Nothing. He rolled right and crawled to the body of one of the gun monkeys, taking the man's pistol, a firearm in each hand now.

A bump across the room. Miller shot both guns twice. A figure broke cover as the last flash of flame left his weapons. Miller jerked as a salvo cut through him, blood filling his throat. With his last ounce of strength, he lifted both guns once again and fired randomly until the actions locked open. Then his arms dropped, and he moved no more.

Nina stayed low as the last shots smacked into the windows behind her, more glass falling, shards nipping at her legs. She rose as soon as the shooting stopped, hustled over to the figure and shot him once more in the head.

She ran for the patio doors, dodging debris, and raced after Dane.

The running man was fifteen yards ahead, stumbling in the sand.

Dane stopped, took aim and squeezed the trigger. Sand sprayed around the man and he dropped. Dane ran, his lungs bursting, legs sore, but he had the quarry he wanted.

Perry Royce scrambled for his fallen gun, grabbing for it as Dane reached him. Dane kicked the gun away. Dane kicked him in the stomach, and Royce doubled up.

The helicopter roared overhead, flying low. Dane ducked instinctively. Royce wasn't beaten yet and lashed out with a kick that sent Dane tumbling into the sand. Royce jumped up and ran for the chopper, waving his arms. The chopper stopped and rotated, turning back to land. A door gunner leaned out and fired. Dane rolled away as the shots ripped into the sand. He took out the .45. Royce was only a few feet away from the flying machine. Dane fired once, twice. The door gunner responded, and Dane rolled toward the ocean and the firm, water-packed sand. He fired again. Royce didn't fall but instead jumped into the helicopter, which quickly began to rise.

Dane gained his feet and ran after the chopper, ocean water lapping at his feet. He fired as he ran, his shots scattered, but the chopper didn't waver. His last round left the muzzle, and the slide locked open. Dane threw the gun and screamed as the helicopter soared over the ocean.

He dropped to his hands and knees, gasping. Soon he heard the chopper no more, just the rhythm of the waves.

Royce had escaped. Dane fell forward on his hands, sinking his fingertips into the sand and squeezing his fists hard. Clenching his teeth, he felt heat in his neck and cheeks. He wanted to yell but the rage stayed inside of him.

Nina found him there.

She knelt beside him and touched his back.

"Don't!"

Nina raised her voice over the ocean waves. "We can't stay here."

Dane squeezed his eyes shut.

"Steve, come on. We have to go." She put her arms around him and started pulling. Finally, he let go of the sand and rose with her. They took two steps and Dane stopped, turning to look into the dark sky where the chopper had gone.

"We haven't lost anything, Steve."

"I'm not giving up," he said.

"Move it," Nina said. "Now!"

Dane didn't stand still any longer. Nina ran ahead of him, and he hustled to keep pace, pushing the defeat from his mind and focusing on the plan.

George DeRocca was next on the hit list.

Chapter Twenty-Six

It wasn't a long flight to Atlantic City, and when the pilot announced their final descent, Dane tightened his seat belt and woke Nina. She'd slept during the whole flight. She stretched and yawned.

"I'm finding it hard to take seriously," he said to her, "the place that Monopoly was based on."

"Look at it this way. If we fail here, we do not pass Go or collect two hundred dollars."

Dane chuckled. "You played Monopoly in Russia?"

"Yes, but it was a little different."

"How?"

"You went to the Gulag instead of jail and the government took everything you built."

Their jet touched down at Atlantic City International, and they collected their luggage and secured a car before checking in at the Cota Hotel & Resort. Right on the beach. Dane knew the rundown of the place from Gallagher's laptop files. It was the hotel George DeRocca ran and it wasn't the only Atlantic City operation the denizens of Operation Eagle controlled. The contraband Dane suspected they trafficked into and around the country stemmed from a food distribution center on 28th Avenue near the John F. Kennedy Memorial Bridge.

Dane had a plan that would give them an up-close look, but they were on borrowed time. Starting yesterday.

They checked in using their own names. There was no reason not to and Dane liked the psychological component. He was throwing his presence in DeRocca's face. He didn't ask for a large suite but a regular room instead. Nina gave him a look. She was not pleased. In the elevator he said they wouldn't be there long enough to enjoy the extra space of a suite.

"All these hotels look the same, you know," Nina said. She placed her bags on the bed in their suite.

Dane opened the window and let in the ocean sounds. The air smelled fresh, without a hint of seaweed or salt. The walls and carpet were different shades of brown, and a large-screen television on the wall faced the beds.

"I need a shower." Nina opened her suitcase and took out fresh clothes.

"I'm going to have a look around while you do that."

"Don't kill anybody without me." Nina started for the bathroom.

Dane stood at the window and waited for the shower to start before making his exit.

Check-in clerks were busy with a long line of guests. Music played from overhead speakers, an up-tempo electronic dance mix that Dane found odd to hear in a place he figured would choose classical music for its atmosphere. Families with little kids, business execs, solo travelers, all moved through the lobby with a mix of excitement, confusion or wariness. As Dane crept through the crowded lobby, his shoes tapping on the tiled floor, he spotted a door marked Private behind the bank of check-in windows.

He turned sharply and went outside. The overcast sky and wind made it a chilly expedition around the perimeter of the building. A vehicle sat in almost every parking stall. New arrivals circled in futility trying to find a spot; he watched them go back out to the street and park off the road.

He walked around to the rear of the building, where a sign that said Staff Only Beyond This Point marked a boundary of sorts, beyond which was another, smaller parking lot with a line of reserved slots up against the rear entrance. A high-end car sat in each spot with a posted sign identifying the spot's exclusive owner.

George DeRocca's silver Mercedes, the windows tinted, sat directly in front of the back door. Dane examined the lock. Heavy deadbolt and standard knob. Nothing he couldn't pick, but the camera in the overhang of the roof said he was not only already under surveillance but faced more fancy security beyond the door.

Dane waved at the camera.

The hotel security crew would report him, of course, maybe even show his face to the boss. He was, in fact, surprised that DeRocca's car was still there. Or the man could have evacuated by another route. He might be thousands of miles away by now, and Dane was chasing a vapor trail.

Only one way to know for sure.

Dane re-entered by a side door and returned to his room. Nina was still in the bathroom, wrapped in a towel and blow-drying her hair. She shut off the dryer. "What did you find?"

"DeRocca's car and I waved to a security camera."

Dane pulled Gallagher's captured Dell laptop out of his

suitcase and set it up on the table by the window. As the sounds of the ocean filtered through the screen, he opened an email from Lukavina. Blueprints of the hotel. As Dane examined the blueprints, Nina, dressed now, came over and sat on the arm of the chair.

"Where did you get those?"

"Len sent them. They're a bit outdated." He pointed out some sections. "They've added here and here, but the main buildings are the same. See this notation? I thought DeRocca's office was on the ground floor, because there's a door marked private behind the check-in desk." He tapped the screen. "He's up at the top of the building instead."

"So, what's the plan?"

"Oh, it's a good one. I repel into DeRocca's office while you're blowing up some trucks."

Dane pulled out his Buck knife and Zippo lighter from a pocket. He placed them on the table.

"That's all you'll need."

"I have to improvise?"

"We don't have time to mess around. We strike tonight. You can get the job done with those."

"I'll do what I can."

"I need a little more conviction than that."

She stood, cleared her throat and pushed out her chest. "I will blow the target to kingdom come."

Dane couldn't keep the smile off his face.

"The chaos I create will make the earth move."

He frowned. "I thought that was my job."

She smacked the back of his head. He laughed.

"Your mood is improving," she said, taking his lighter and knife and sitting on the bed.

Dane pushed back from the table and crossed his legs. "I think I've come to terms with everything. Now I just want to tear the world apart."

"Or somebody's world."

Dane nodded.

"What else do I need to know?"

"Look for the trucks with the blue stripes."

"Why?"

"Gallagher's notes say those are the ones with the contraband and the gun crews."

"Gun crews?"

"Nothing you can't handle."

She shook her head. "This information is how old?"

"Almost a decade."

"They could have changed," she said.

"Then check before you use the Zippo."

"How about we change parts?"

"No. I have some words for DeRocca. As you can imagine."

Dane closed the laptop.

Chapter Twenty-Seven

A long guard with a silenced submachine gun wandered the roof, the bright lights of Atlantic City on one side and the black void of the ocean on the other. The breeze carried a salty wetness now; he tasted the salt on his lips. He went to the edge and looked down. DeRocca's balcony waited below. A pool of light from the office spilled onto the bare patio.

There had been a lot of private meetings and quiet phone calls over the past few days. The guard and his compatriots knew something bad was happening, but DeRocca hadn't filled them in. All they knew was that they had to be extra sharp until further notice. The trooper would have preferred somebody on the roof with him, but he had a radio on his belt to reach the crew in an emergency.

The guard walked the perimeter once again. DeRocca's troops covered the roof in two-hour shifts. It was one of the dullest duties one could pull and the guard still had ninety minutes to go. All he wanted was to get back inside where it was warm and well lit.

The guard stopped at the edge above DeRocca's balcony and shifted the sling attached to his weapon.

The roof door opened with a squeak.

The guard turned, bringing up the stubby submachine gun. He never heard the shot that killed him.

Dane wore a rappelling harness under his jacket, a coil of rope around his chest. There was a silencer attached to the Detonics Scoremaster in his right hand. He advanced carefully up the stairwell, the roof door looming above. At the landing he tested the knob. It turned easily, but the hinges let off a whine that might have been heard in Cleveland. The door was heavy steel, and he stayed low, using it as a partial shield, as he moved onto the roof. Nothing on his right.

He looked around the door. The trooper at the edge of the roof raised his weapon. Dane fired once. The .45 sounded like a heavy book being dropped on a desk. The slug struck the guard in the center of his chest and the man fell forward in a heap. Dane ran over and shot him again in the head. He dropped into a squat, pivoting 360 degrees. No other guards. The dead man had a radio on his belt. The numbers started falling in Dane's head. As soon as the guard missed his check-in, the alert would go out. The tough part was, Dane had no idea how long he had before that happened.

He holstered the .45, took off his coat, and uncoiled the rope and anchored it to an air conditioner. The rest he fed through the rappelling hook on his harness.

The harness, called a Swiss seat, looked like a Speedo made of rope. The rope ran between his legs and around his backside and caused an embarrassing bulge in front. There was no way to look cool wearing one. Luckily it disengaged easily.

Dane dropped over the side and let gravity carry him

into space. His pulse quickened as he dangled like a spider on the end of a web. He fed the rope through gloved hands, descending slowly toward the balcony. He swayed with the wind, his stomach lurching every time.

Maybe Nina had a better job after all, but he needed to face DeRocca. The man had maintained a friendship with Dane's father more than anybody else at CIA. Dane remembered his smile and favorite beer. His old man had kept the brand around specifically for him.

And now Dane had a bullet specifically for him.

George DeRocca adjusted his bifocals and read the latest email from the distribution site.

The patio window was open a crack to let in fresh air, but he kept snapping nervous eyes at the glass despite the security on the roof and elsewhere in the building. Royce had been very clear what was happening, and who was causing it, and DeRocca was the last line of defense between Royce, Lassen and everything they had worked to accomplish. He wanted to leave the country with Royce, but that wasn't possible. Weapons still needed to get from the US to San Remo to keep the military supplied so they could fight the rebels.

DeRocca needed to make sure the gear arrived complete and intact, otherwise Steve Dane was the least of their problems.

But Royce had told him Lassen's alternate plan, as well. Using him as bait.

He didn't like that very much but accepted it as part of the business. All he had to do was wait, and Lassen's crew would take care of the rest. They were already at the hotel, scouting for the arrival of Dane and the woman.

Back to the email. The information in the text updated

the truck departure schedule for the evening. They were ahead by an hour. Not too bad. As soon as the guns and equipment were on the road, DeRocca had his own private escape plan all ready to execute.

DeRocca had wanted only to serve his country from his days in the Navy to when he'd joined the CIA. His friendship with Royce, and the promise of more money than they could ever earn honestly, had taken him down this admittedly dangerous path. Now the past was coming back to haunt them. Taking out Richard Dane had been one thing; they never should have left his kid alive. But Royce had thought he knew better. So much for the brains of the outfit.

A rush of wind rustled papers on his desk. He slapped the pages down. Movement in the shadows. He turned his head. A man framed in the patio doorway covered him with a pistol. A shot would hit him in the chest dead center.

"Don't move, George."

Dane approached the desk.

"Hands flat."

"You've sure grown up."

"Don't start."

DeRocca put both hands on the desk, fingers splayed. DeRocca peeked over the frame of his bifocals at the unwavering snout of the stainless Detonics .45. Dane did not relax his aim.

DeRocca said, "I should have known you'd get through."

"If there's a party planned for me, I might be a little late."

"How did you put it all together?"

"You can blame Gallagher. Attack of conscience. Plus, I have his files. All of them."

"Lassen said Gallagher would be a problem. Royce and I disagreed."

"Who is Lassen?"

DeRocca laughed. "You still don't have the whole story."

"You want to make a deal? Escape the gallows and live out your years in Florida? Look at me, George. Do you think that's going to happen? You know what happened to Gallagher."

DeRocca swallowed hard.

"Listen, I voted against what happened to your father—"

"Don't lie to me."

"I'll tell you everything. Turn me over to the Feds. I'll talk to Congress. We'll blow Eagle wide open."

"We have the files. That means we don't need you."

DeRocca sighed. "Then you might as well shoot me."

Dane slipped his finger back onto the trigger.

The phone rang.

"Answer. We don't want anybody to think something is wrong."

DeRocca picked up the phone.

Chapter Twenty-Eight

Nina lay in the shadows, dressed head to toe in black. DeRocca's distribution center sat across the street, floodlights filling the area with brightness. Through binoculars she examined the east side of the building.

The complex covered an entire square block. The loading area for departing semis was on the east side. Thirty semis sat in a line at the docks. On the southern end of the building, more semis were parked side by side.

The east-side trucks took priority, she figured. They were marked as Dane had described.

Nina put away the binoculars and checked her 9-millimeter. The S&W pistol had a full magazine plus one in the chamber.

She picked a spot near the fence where the floodlights didn't penetrate because of a big-rig wash station. Nina scaled the fence in three strides and landed on the hard blacktop opposite. The wash station was high and long, room for three rigs total, and she dropped flat to examine the ground ahead.

The floodlights were aimed at the trucks on the east

side of the warehouse. That left the blacktop between the building and Nina open and in the dark. There were one or two places she could hide on the other side, but the lights would make long-term hiding very difficult.

She grumbled to herself about the assignment, but Steve thought it was important. Time to get to work.

Nina ran at full speed across the blacktop. She aimed for the corner of the building and a stack of pallets. It would put her mere feet from the first big rig. Her feet and legs felt the impact each time her shoes landed, her lungs beginning to burn. She reached the pallets and dropped flat.

A golf cart rattled around the corner, the two men aboard stopping in front of the rig nearest Nina. She remained facedown and flat.

The rig's cabin door swung open and she peeked: Two men were inspecting the rig, one on the outside checking underneath with a flashlight, the other in the cabin. This second man opened a compartment in the door and checked the load in a short machine pistol. He returned the weapon to the compartment.

What contraband was so valuable that they needed armed crews?

The two inspectors moved to the next rig down the line, but Nina stayed in place. She needed them to get farther away, but the longer she stayed where she was, the greater the chance of discovery.

By the time the inspectors reached the fifth rig, she had crawled to the first.

She slid under the rig and felt along the top of the side-mounted gas tank. The fuel line started on top of the tank, a thick stainless-steel tube, and it was attached to another hose, this one rubber and encased by a steel mesh wrap, clamped at either end. She worked the screws with a Leatherman tool. She pulled the mesh away and placed it on the ground. Using Dane's Buck knife, she sliced open the rubber hose and jerked aside as gas started to dribble out. The fluid smacked the pavement, and a pool started to grow. Nina rolled out from under the rig and crawled to the next one, feeling for the meshed hose once again. The odor of gas filled the air.

She managed the second and third rigs before the inspectors returned. Their voices grew louder as they neared her position under the third rig. She scooted back under the trailer, the puddle of gas widening. Some had already splashed on her outfit. This was not where she wanted to be.

The inspectors stopped and ceased their conversation. "Do you smell gas?"

Nina slipped Dane's Zippo from her back pocket. She carefully opened the flip top to muffle the click.

She edged between two wheels and moved as far back as she could. As the inspectors stepped closer, she snapped the Zippo to life and placed it on the ground. The pool of gas inched closer. Nina cleared the tires and stayed low between the third and fourth rigs, coiled for a sprint back to the fence.

The inspectors started yelling as the puddle of gas caught the Zippo's flame and the fuel ignited with a flash. The inspectors screamed as the flames rushed out from under the cabin. Nina took off like an Olympic sprinter.

Shouts behind her. Crackle of gunfire. Shots nicked the ground near her. She cut left for the wash station. A glance back. Three armed men coming her way. The fire had spread to the other two rigs.

Nina dove into a wash station bay and clawed for the 9-millimeter. She held the gun in her left hand as she leaned out and returned fire, one of the shooters falling while the other two spread out and dropped flat. Nina left the station for the fence, bursts of fire whistling around her. She vaulted the fence and landed hard, bending at the knees to absorb the jolting impact.

She ran for her car.

The fire from the big rigs spread to the warehouse, flames shooting into the sky.

George DeRocca lifted the telephone receiver. Dane's eyes and the snout of his gun never shifted.

"Yes?"

He listened, his eyes widening as he stared at Dane.

"Do what you have to do."

He listened.

"It doesn't matter, Harry."

DeRocca hung up. "Your people?"

"It's over, George. Come around the desk."

DeRocca moved on shaky legs around the desk to the spot on the carpet Dane indicated.

"My men will be on the way up," DeRocca said. "The guard on the roof will have missed his check-in by now."

Dane kicked DeRocca behind one knee, and the older man collapsed, Dane straddling his opponent and leaning down to lift DeRocca's head by pulling his hair.

"Don't do this!" DeRocca hissed out the words, breathing hard.

Dane pressed the .45 into the back of DeRocca's head. The older man sucked air sharply.

"Take it like a man, George. I could make this so much worse."

The office door opened with a crash.

Chapter Twenty-Nine

Two men entered, both armed, both wearing hotel security jackets.

DeRocca let out a shout, but only got half the yell out of his mouth. Dane fired the .45 and blasted most of DeRocca's face and pieces of his skull into the carpet. He swung the .45 to the new arrivals. Three rounds in quick succession. Two missed. The third hit one of the security men and knocked him back into the other. Both tumbled against the hallway wall.

Dane changed magazines and ran for the patio as the second gunman shoved his partner's body aside and ran into the office. Dane fired once. The gunman dived for some furniture. His return shot shattered the patio glass as Dane cleared the doorway. Bits of glass tugged at Dane's clothes and bit the back of his neck.

He cut right, taking cover by the wall, firing into the office as the gunman charged after him. The .45 slugs cut through the man's legs and stomach. The shooter landed on the floor. Dane shot him again.

Dane holstered the Scoremaster, smoothed his jacket and crossed the office. He glanced at DeRocca's body, the pool of blood under his head soaking the carpet. He didn't feel any sense of accomplishment. He didn't feel anything at all. Maybe he would when he caught up with Royce. If he could find him.

He stepped over the dead security man and advanced down the hall. The walls and tiled floor were bare; only the doors of the elevator ahead had any color—brown. He pressed the call button and stood to one side. The doors slid open. Nobody there. He stepped in and pressed the button for the lobby. The doors slid shut and the elevator began its descent.

Dane changed clips again, his last mag, and put the gun back under his jacket. He took a deep breath as the elevator settled on the lobby floor.

He and Nina had arranged a rendezvous. All he had to do was get out of the building. But he rode in DeRocca's private elevator. It would deposit Dane near the check-in desk. If security was nearby, they'd know he didn't belong. Dane cleared his throat, squared his shoulders, and the doors opened.

Dane walked down the hall to the exit and entered the lobby. A line of people stood waiting to check in; two security people standing by a column noticed him right away. One spoke into a radio. Dane winked as he went by. They wouldn't fire on him. Not with the public around. He continued toward the lobby doors. The shield of the public would end as soon as he left the building.

A family entered as Dane exited. He used the family for cover and looked back. The two security men were still on his tail but keeping their distance.

Where was the rest of the force?

Dane crossed the parking lot asphalt and started walking between cars, looking every which way. Then he heard boots pounding on the pavement. A lot of boots.

From the left and right, two separate groups were swarming through the lot, directed by the shouting orders of one man. Dane dropped between two cars. Well, nobody had said escape would be easy.

He looked ahead. Three more rows of cars before he reached the street. The boss of the group told everybody to spread out and search.

Shuffling footsteps froze Dane in place. A man with a radio and pistol approached Dane's spot. Dane jumped up and punched the guard in the throat. He let the man fall and ran to the next row. Somebody yelled. A shot cracked and nicked the heel of Dane's left shoe. Dane stumbled and fell forward, narrowly missing the fender of a sedan. Breath left him on impact. He groaned. Forcing himself up, he continued forward, but then a spotlight found him. Dane drew the .45 and pivoted right. The security man who held the spotlight yelled something. Dane answered with the .45. The man dropped, the light breaking as it hit the ground, and Dane continued forward. Not much farther. He surged ahead to the sidewalk, traffic screeching and drivers honking as he ran across the busy street.

Two blocks to the rendezvous.

He ducked into an alley, gasping, and checked the way he'd come. A pair of black SUVs was pulling out of the parking lot. They probably wanted to set up a perimeter, but any show of force or any clash would certainly bring the cops. Of course, they had to have a plan, or maybe some bought cops, to get around that.

The only good news was that they had no idea where Dane had gone and needed to set up a search pattern.

One of the SUVs sped by the alley and pulled over. The

doors opened and two males climbed out. One crossed the street. How many remained in the vehicle?

Dane walked the length of the alley to the opposite street. Turning left, he stayed close to the wall, hands in his pockets, trying for as casual a profile as possible.

Dane walked down Atlantic Avenue. The bridge on North Albany was the meeting spot. Black SUVs from the hotel continued crisscrossing the streets. Dane did not react. Plenty of pedestrians provided cover.

Atlantic turned into O'Donnell Parkway; Dane took a left on Albany, and the bridge lay ahead. A stalled sedan sat in the right lane. Dane quickened his pace. Nina for sure. It was their rental. He still had his hand on the .45 as he approached, but a peek through the passenger window confirmed it was Nina behind the wheel.

He opened the door and dropped in beside her.

She started the car and continued across the bridge. Filbert Avenue ahead.

"So?" he said.

"I should have brought marshmallows."

"Good." Dane took out his phone.

"DeRocca?"

"Dead." Dane dialed.

Nina stopped for a light.

"Len, it's Dane," he said into the phone. "Check out DeRocca's trucking company, like we talked about. They had a fire tonight."

Nina drove across the intersection.

"I'm sure you'll find—"

Nina screamed as the bright lights of an SUV filled the car. The SUV rammed the rental just behind Nina's seat. Glass shattered and metal crunched as the impact shoved the rental across the intersection, where another SUV collided on Dane's side.

Gun crews leaped out of the SUVs and hauled Dane and Nina out of the rental and loaded them each into one of the SUVs, the big vehicles with their now damaged front ends pulling away in opposite directions.

Chapter Thirty

Dane felt a dull throb, and then heard it. The drone was a constant low note. He opened his eyes. The surrounding light hurt his eyes, but he forced them open anyway. The cabin of a private jet, the sunshade to his left wide open. He couldn't lift his head. His hands were cuffed behind his back, his ankles shackled to the floor.

He managed to roll his head right. Nina, similarly bound, sat across the aisle. She was unconscious and drooling on her outfit. She'd get a kick out of that later.

Two gunmen sat up front. One rose and knocked on the cockpit door, spoke to the man who answered and led him to Dane.

Dane swallowed. His throat felt like sandpaper. He did not know the man standing before him. He had puffy black hair, dark skin, a mole on his chin. Dane mentally christened him Mole Man until further notice. Or The Molenator. Molenofski.

"Did you have a nice nap, Mr. Dane?"

"I've been drugged."

"You were. Your lady, too."

"Who are you?"

"I am Sanchez. I am taking you to my employer."

"Where?"

"San Remo."

"Never heard of her," Dane said.

Sanchez grinned. "Very funny, Mr. Dane. You will enjoy our country, what little you'll see of it before we drop you and your lady in a grave."

"Why go through the trouble? You had us dead to rights."

"My employer will tell you. He has his reason for doing it this way."

Mole Man returned to the cockpit, and Dane was left in the presence of knocked-out Nina and two armed troops, and he couldn't move with his wrists and ankles shackled.

He turned to Nina. The drool stain on her top extended two inches from the collar.

At least he had something to laugh at.

The change in altitude combined with his ears popping meant they were about to land.

Nina stirred and lifted her head. Her disorientation didn't last long, and when her eyes found Dane, he smiled.

"What are you so happy about?" she said.

"We're alive and about to meet the enemy. Think of all the extra work we won't have to do."

Nina groaned and turned away. "I think I liked it better when you were dark and brooding."

Presently the wheels chirped as the jet touched down, and Sanchez supervised while the troopers unshackled Dane and Nina.

San Remo. Dane had indeed heard of the country sometime in the past. Small nation in Central America, close to

Venezuela. Forgotten by most of the world, since it didn't have oil or grow tobacco or sugar. Or much of anything. San Remo just sort of existed.

He figured he'd learn a whole lot more about the place shortly. Perhaps on San Remo they'd find Royce's international benefactor.

A white Chevy Tahoe with police markings waited at the bottom of the exit stairs. Sanchez and his troops loaded Dane and Nina into the back. The uniformed officer behind the wheel drove away. No customs and a police escort. Sanchez's employer had connections.

They drove along the side of the runway. Dane noted no jumbo jets, just smaller Lears and Cessna Citations—the air force of the cartels and other members of the ungodly. Dane also noticed the absence of a control tower. This was a private airfield that didn't see a lot of use.

The cop left the airport through an electric gate and turned onto the road. No lane lines but plenty of space for opposing traffic, of which they saw none for the next twenty minutes up a winding mountain road with lush green forest on either side. Then the road flattened, some of the forest fell away, and they followed the road around the side of the mountain.

Dane exchanged a glance with Nina. She shrugged. The further they traveled the more complicated escape became.

"Hey, Sanchez," Dane said, "are we there yet?"

The burly man with the mole didn't bother to look back.

Eventually the Tahoe stopped in front of an arched marble gate, opened by an armed guard. The SUV drove through. The access road led to the front of a mansion. Steps led to the front doors; the wide porch overhang supported by thick columns.

A tall man with dark hair stood alone by one of the

columns.

The Tahoe stopped in front of the steps. Sanchez and his troops exited first, then helped out Dane and Nina, who were marched up the steps to where the tall man waited.

Dane met the man's blue-eyed gaze. He had the sharp jaw and high cheekbones. He wore a white suit, with a sparkling Rolex. Dane noted a diamond ring. The man liked to wear some of his wealth.

"Hello, Mr. Dane."

"Hello."

"Have a problem on the plane, Ms. Talikova?"

"Huh?"

Dane said, "You drooled on your top, honey."

Nina looked and brushed at the wet stain. "How lovely."

The tall man looked at Dane. "Pardon me if don't shake hands."

"Pardon me if I don't care. Who are you?"

"Gallagher's notes didn't include me?"

"No. But the CIA knows you exist."

The tall man smiled. "My name is Cyrus Lassen. For now, that's all you need to know. Sanchez will escort you to your room. You will have a short stay, but I am not a poor host in spite of these circumstances. My home is well guarded. There is no way out and jungle all around. You will not leave until I say so, and then you'll have two dozen troops with dogs on your trail."

"What does that mean?"

"You'll see."

Lassen snapped an order at Sanchez. Sanchez and the troops shoved Dane and Nina into the house. Dane looked back before the big oak doors shut. Lassen remained by the column, staring into the distance. He was a man with a lot on his mind.

Sanchez showed Dane and Nina to a large and well-decorated bedroom on the fourth floor. He closed the door behind them. The lock snapped in place with a light click.

Dane looked around. Plush carpet. Canopy bed. Curtains across the windows. Art on the walls and antique knickknacks displayed on shelves.

"Expect bugs and cameras," Dane said.

Nina pulled open the curtains to find another curtain of razor wire outside the window, followed by a steep drop to the patio four floors below.

"No exit this way," she said, "even if I grew out my hair."

"Just relax, Rapunzel."

Dane found clothes in the closet that looked like their sizes. A desk by the bed showed a handful of Montecristo Habana cigars and a bottle of Glenfiddich.

"Could be poisoned," Nina said.

"Nobody is going to poison Cuban Montecristos or twenty-year-old Scotch," Dane said. "That's inhuman."

Dane climbed onto the bed and stretched out.

"Are you serious?"

"Come and lie down, babe. There's no sense trying to find a way out of here just yet. We could use a nap."

"I've slept enough."

"Afraid of drooling again?"

Nina let out a curse and went into the bathroom. She closed the door extra hard.

Dane dozed off almost immediately.

Chapter Thirty-One

Dane woke up and suggested they get dressed for dinner. Nina, frustrated with her outfit, cursed as she stood in front of the bathroom mirror.

"That looks good on you," Dane said.

Nina tightened the belt. "Pants are too big and too short."

The cuffs of the trousers stopped just above her ankles.

The shirt Dane wore was also a bit tight, and the sleeves were short. He stared at his fire-scarred right arm and something smoldered deep within him. He knew psychological warfare when he saw it. A good operative would ignore such things. The fact that he was even thinking about it told Dane the trick might be working. Lassen knew more than Dane had thought he did.

Somebody knocked on the door. It opened and Sanchez came in.

"Dinner is ready," Sanchez said.

"This is the presidential retreat, if you didn't know," Lassen said. "*El Presidente* and I have an arrangement."

Cyrus Lassen sat at the head of the table, Sanchez at the other end; Dane and Nina sat across from each other. A centerpiece of lilies divided them.

The servers cleared the salad dishes and promptly returned with steak and garlic mashed potatoes.

"I figured you'd enjoy a good steak," Lassen said, sipping a glass of red wine. "Seeing it's your last meal and all that."

Dane cut into the meat and chewed a bite. "My compliments. This is perfect."

Lassen offered a grin, laughing with his eyes.

"So, this is a perfect place to hide out?" Dane said.

"Yes. I provide certain services to the government and in exchange I get to stay here."

"Let me guess. Royce and his gang eliminated the enemies of El Presidente, right?"

Lassen shrugged. "Not quite. We have our share of problems in this country, a certain band of rebels trying to get rid of President Marco."

"They've been fighting a long time?"

"Not quite." Lassen smiled. "Not much at all, really."

"And that's why Royce was moving guns and money and equipment down here to help the government fight. Why does Royce care what happens here?"

"You'll have to ask him," Lassen said.

"Except it's not hard to answer. San Remo is the anonymous country. Royce linked up with the Mafia. It's the perfect spot to hide money and fugitives and make it into a nice criminal sanctuary. All with government approval."

"So you say."

"What do you get in return?"

"What do you think?"

"Intelligence information?"

"And other things," Lassen said.

Dane nodded ate some more, chewing slowly as he further examined the man in the white suit. Nina watched him.

"You don't seem to think the rebels are much of a threat," Dane said. "Why?"

Lassen said, "The rebels are not of much concern. They are small and unorganized. You won't find any help there, if that's what you're thinking."

Dane offered no reply.

"The only thing you will find in San Remo is your death. Starting tonight. You two run. We chase. Stay alive as long as you can. Eventually we will get you."

"Sounds like a story I read in high school," Dane said. "I should start calling you Zaroff."

"There won't be a wager in this case," Lassen said. "Very poetic. Almost ironic."

"I don't know what you mean."

"We both have a reason for wanting to kill each other. Our paths have been on a collision course for a long time."

Dane frowned. "I've never heard of you until now."

"Does somebody named the Duchess mean anything to you?"

"I knew Angelica Kyznetsov for a short time, yes."

Lassen lifted his wineglass. "She was my wife."

Dane remembered her well. An international arms dealer of some renown who had found a way to buy a nuclear weapon and almost did, until Dane interrupted the sale. When he and Nina finally tracked her down, the battle had been intense but brief, and the Duchess hadn't walked away.

Dane kept his eyes on Lassen. "You and Royce killed my father; I killed your wife. Very interesting."

"We're both suitably fueled to see the other destroyed."

"You should have heard your wife scream when my grenade ripped her in half."

Lassen pushed his plate away, his jaw clenched tight. He snapped his fingers. "You've had enough."

The servers removed Dane's and Nina's plates. Lassen and Dane did not break eye-contact.

"You'll be chasing us, too?" Dane said.

"No."

"Others do your dirty work for you?"

"It's the best way," Lassen said. "Why get my hands dirty? This is how you stay off the radar and never get caught. If you get a second life, you might want to consider it. You two could live longer."

Dane started out of his seat, but strong hands grabbed him, forcing him back. The burly man with the mole stood above him.

"I'm dealing with this one?" Dane said to Lassen.

Lassen gave an exaggerated nod.

"I'm going to kill him like I killed your wife, Cyrus."

"We'll see."

Lassen made a gesture with his left hand. Sanchez lifted Dane out of the chair and forced him out of the room, another trooper prodding Nina as well. She followed behind Dane without protest.

At the door, Dane stole a glance back at Lassen.

The man in white sat calmly at the table, contemplating the sparkle of his diamond ring.

Sanchez wore black, including black jungle boots, with a pistol on his hip, as he and ten troopers armed with automatic weapons escorted Dane and Nina to the edge of the property's west side. They filed through a gate in the wall. Twenty paces later, they reached the beginning of the forest.

The night sounds were well underway, filling the darkness ahead with a sense of doom. Dane couldn't see five feet in front of him.

Dane's pulse quickened. Nina took his hand and squeezed.

Sanchez and the troops stopped.

Dane's eyes bounced around the grim faces of the troops. He gripped Nina's hand tightly. The minutes dragged by as the night's chill bit at Dane's arms and face. Crickets chirped; other animal sounds drifted through the darkness. Dane and Nina faced danger from man and beast.

They did not speak. The troopers were obviously waiting for Lassen. Lassen's footsteps reached them first, his shoes landing hard on the soft ground.

"Are we ready?" Lassen said.

He stopped beside Sanchez. He smiled at Dane.

"You will have a half hour head start," Lassen said. "Better not waste it."

"Be seeing you," Dane said. He led Nina into the dark forest.

They had not even a hint of moonlight to help. Wet leaves smacked at them; branches scraped and prodded. Dane kept hold of Nina's hand, their palms sweaty. They breathed heavily, forcing through the foliage, feeling around tree trunks and fallen logs.

"They're gonna start early," Nina said.

"They're not chasing us in the dark."

"You don't think so?"

Dane laughed. "They're going to get a night's sleep and let us scare ourselves half to death in the dark. Come on."

At each tree they found, Dane felt around the trunk with his free hand.

"What are you doing?"

"We need a place to hole up."

"What if they bring dogs?"

"Then we're finished. But not till daylight."

"We might be finished anyway."

"Now is not the time to be a Debbie Downer."

"I need a drink," Nina said.

Another fallen trunk blocked them, the soft ground and wet foliage entangling their feet as they followed the length to the other end. They continued forward, Dane pulling her close, grunting as more leaves snapped at them.

"Let's stop a second," Nina said.

"Our only chance is distance," Dane said. "And hiding till daylight."

"Where?"

Dane found another tree trunk and felt around. Another solid log.

"Anywhere," he said, moving on.

Chapter Thirty-Two

Dane's feet caught on a stump. He fell hard. He breathed heavily into the wet dirt.

Nina landed beside him. "Are you hurt?" She felt his arms and legs. "Steve?"

"Just winded," he said between breaths.

"Let's stay here. Just a minute."

"Good idea."

"How do we get through this?"

"We'll think of something."

"You always have a plan," she said.

"Maybe we can find the rebels."

"That's a long shot."

"It's all I got, honey. They have to be watching Lassen's place. It would be a primary target."

"I hope you're right."

Dane started to rise. Nina found his left hand and helped him up.

"Come on," he said.

They started forward again.

Later, Dane and Nina found a tree and dropped flat

behind it. Their clothes were wet with sweat and mud. Eventually they blended with the jungle. Insects buzzed. The night breeze rustled leaves. Creatures scurried. No sign of larger two-legged creatures.

Dane used both hands to brush as much debris away from the tree as he could, creating a flat space. "Try to get a little sleep," Dane said.

"That's impossible."

"Just try."

She burrowed close but they still shivered. Daylight couldn't come fast enough. Maybe then they'd have a chance. They held each other tight to take advantage of body heat.

The sun finally cut through the jungle canopy around 7 a.m. The eyes that watched Dane and Nina from twenty yards away belonged not to one of Lassen's hunters, but to a twelve-year-old boy named Paco Gomez.

His hair was buzz-cut close his skull. He wore jungle camouflage, black boots, with camo paint on his face. He clutched a US M-16 rifle.

Paco was in the vicinity of the Gringo Dragon's home against his father's orders. His father, Roberto, leader of the Sons of San Remo, did not want Paco to leave camp. But Paco needed to find out what had happened to his Uncle Rico. His uncle and two others had gone to try and kill the Gringo Dragon, only to not return.

Paco's father said that meant Rico had been killed.

Paco wasn't convinced, so he left camp to find the answers.

Instead, he spotted two others, a white male and female, hiding in the forest not far from the Dragon's castle.

He kept watch. Maybe they were friendly. Maybe they knew what happened to Uncle Rico.

Nina nudged Dane. He awoke with a start, coughing into his hand. He looked at her.

"You okay?"

"Must look like hell."

"We both do."

"You're supposed to say the opposite, ass."

Dane looked at their muddy clothes. He dug up a handful of dirt and smeared it on his bare arms and face. "Copy me. We need all the camo we can get now that the sun is up."

Nina followed his example.

"You were right, they've left us alone out here," she said, bits of mud falling from one cheek.

"Told you. Playing head games. They're on the move now, though."

"We need to find a broken branch, preferably thick, preferably a pair."

"You read my mind, baby."

They left the tree in search of anything that might make a temporary weapon. Dane had visions of capturing a firearm. Preferably one with a lot of bullets in the magazine.

The ground remained flat, the brush thick, the forest overgrown as far as their eyes could see.

They moved slowly. Only their breathing mingled with the morning sounds of chirping birds and the occasional call of an animal. Any creatures in the vicinity were keeping their distance from the two-legged, mud-smeared animals.

Nina stepped ahead of Dane, Dane grabbing her right arm to pull her back. She reacted with a gasp. Dane pointed at the ground.

"Right there."

"What?"

"Trip wire. Light hit it just right."

Dane dropped into a crouch and scooted closer. The wire was between two tree trunks and heavily concealed by forest debris. If the sunlight hadn't winked off the steel wife, they'd have walked right into it.

Dane told Nina to stand still. On his hands and knees, negotiating the natural obstacles that stabbed into his palms and knees, he followed the tripwire to one end where it was roped around a tree trunk. No explosive on that side. He retraced to the other end, and found the wire wrapped around another trunk, with one end plugged into a black box at the base of the tree.

The box was not a Claymore or a grenade or anything he'd ever associate with a tripwire.

Rejoining Nina, he explained nothing as he found a jagged branch with peeling bark and dropped it on the tripwire.

The wire snapped.

"No bomb?" Nina said.

A motor whirred. Dane and Nina looked up. It took a few minutes, both remaining in place, and then they saw the video camera mounted under a tree branch, the lens zeroed where they were standing.

"Battery operated cameras," he said. "Whoever is on the other end of us knows our exact position. The tripwire activated a location unit. It's probably lighting up a board back at the house."

"We should run," she said.

"We should run really fast," Dane said.

They broke into a sprint and put that place behind them.

They did not forget the main objective as they hurried.

After several tries, they finally found branches that made worthwhile weapons, as long as they somehow came up behind any of Lassen's troopers. Branches weren't bulletproof, a deficiency perhaps the Creator would correct the next time He designed a planet. Perhaps He'd let Dane consult.

They moved in bursts, the light a great help but the steaming humidity making it hard to move often. Their clothes were soaked; the mud so carefully applied to skin to hide them now dripped in yucky brown trails down their faces, arms and legs.

Dane held up a hand as they moved along a trail. Nina froze. Dane stopped flat and Nina followed. She crawled beside him.

"I saw something," he said.

"What?"

"The ground isn't right. See that patch of brush? We're about to fall into a pit."

Dane rose and approached the area of concern, stabbing at it right his branch. The brush fell away sharply, landing on something below. He swept the remaining cover away and looked down on a set of six sharp steel spikes that were waiting for a body.

The partial remains of a body were already at the bottom of the pit.

"Poor chap," Dane said.

Nina joined him but made no comment.

"Lassen has a lot to answer for," Dane said. "Keep moving."

He nudged Nina around the pit and they continued forward.

"Helicopter!" Nina said.

Dane stopped and listened. The whipping rotor blades were unmistakable.

"Arriving at our last position," Dane said.

"We aren't far enough away."

"Then shift gears and run, baby, run!"

Dane and Nina ran a short distance before Nina tripped and fell headlong into the brush, letting out a scream. She recoiled back, slapping at her clothes. Blood from her hands mixed with the mud already there.

"Are you hurt?"

"There's another body!"

Dane moved the brush aside and winced. This was a fresh kill, the poor bastard shot through, his eyes tightly shut. A dog tag dangled from his neck. Dane looked at the ID plate.

Rico Gomez. Captain. Blood A+. Catholic.

He yanked the chain from the dead man's neck and stowed it in a pocket. Should they find any rebels, they might want to know one of their captains had died.

"Any weapons?" Nina said.

"No. Looks like his fingers were broken. He had something and they had to work very hard to get it from him."

"We have to stop what's happening here," Nina said.

"It's what we do, baby."

Dane started forward again.

Chapter Thirty-Three

Leaves rustled in the distance. Behind cover, Dane tried to discern movement. Nothing. They waited. An eternity passed.

More rustling, ahead and to the right. This time Dane didn't have to try to see.

"Three of them," Nina said.

He concurred. Three troopers armed with Heckler & Koch UMP submachine guns. Dane almost salivated at the sight. He longed for one of those weapons the way he might want a steak and a cigar.

"Let them pass," he said.

The troops stomped through the foliage with ease, heads moving side to side. They had no fear of being shot. They figured the quarry would be tired, scared, hiding like rabbits. Dane grinned. They didn't know him or Nina at all.

The troopers passed. They at least marched properly, in a V formation, with plenty of distance between them.

"They must have broken into small units like this," Nina said. "They'll be everywhere."

"Uh-huh." Dane rose slowly. Time for the hunted to become the hunter. They moved at a half crouch, keeping about twenty meters behind the three troopers. Dane's legs began to scream from the strain, but they soon closed the gap and Dane struck first.

They leaped from the half crouch, and he swung his club at the trooper at the right rear position of the V, swinging the club as hard as he could. The other two didn't know he was there until the club broke against the trooper's skull with a sharp crack. The trooper let out a yell as Dane tackled him. They were swallowed by the foliage, which rustled as they struggled.

Nina appeared and smacked the second trooper, her branch not breaking but instead landing with a solid thunk that turned the trooper's legs to jelly. He fell where he stood.

The last man started to run for cover. Dane and Nina jumped up again almost at the same time with HKs at their shoulders. The SMGs crackled. The third trooper dropped as the bullets stitched through his back.

Dane and Nina launched into action without words. They stripped the troopers of ammunition, canteens and ration packs. The troopers' camo jackets were also a good prize, though Nina had to roll the sleeves above her wrist. The combat harnesses fit better and had the spare ammo and water, of which they drank several mouthfuls.

"Big improvement," Dane said.

Nina moved past him. He followed, HK cocked and locked. She pushed through some leaves. A spot on the ground showed footprints.

"I saw somebody move from here," she said. She knelt down and examined the prints. "Did you see any midgets at Lassen's?"

"They prefer the term 'little people,' dear."

"These are not adult-sized footprints."

Dane looked and agreed. He spun around, scanning the distance. "Hear that?"

"Dogs," she said.

"We gotta move."

Dane and Nina powered through the foliage, dodging and leaping over obstacles, the sudden incline of the ground making the rush more difficult. The incline sharpened, Nina tripping, Dane helping her up. Almost breathless, they continued, Dane's lungs burning from the strain.

The high ground might help if it meant seeing troops or dogs from a distance. A massive hollowed-out tree stump, the rest of the towering mass long gone, loomed ahead. "Go for that!" Dane rasped. They hustled. The inside of the trunk offered them a small fortress, albeit one that wasn't bulletproof.

Dane and Nina rolled over the side and into the hollow center, lying on the jagged and rough remains, gasping. Dane struggled to lean against the trunk wall and peek over the edge. The seat of leaves rustled with a soft breeze.

Nina propped herself up beside him. She swallowed some water. "How long?"

"Anytime."

Dane checked the HK. It was chambered for 9-millimeter. Perfect if you wanted to get up close but not the best for distance shooting. They'd have to wait until the enemy neared.

"Shoot carefully," he said. "Don't go full auto until they're in front of us."

"You sound like this is our Alamo."

"Hell, it's our Bastogne."

The barking grew in volume, sharp and aggressive, and Dane moved his eyes back and forth, searching for movement.

Twelve-year-old Paco Gomez chewed a meal bar. He was hiding be-hind a stump not far from the man and woman. They were on the run from the Gringo Dragon's troops, and he didn't understand why, but they could fight and knew their weapons, and that meant his father would want to know as much about them as Paco could learn. Maybe he might be able to bring them to camp.

Paco swallowed the last of the meal bar and checked his rifle. Magazine locked, round in the chamber. He had two grenades within easy reach. He heard the dogs approaching. They could find him as easily as the man and woman. That made him nervous. But they also might confuse the scents and become disoriented. That might work to the man and woman's advantage.

The barking grew louder, the dogs visible now, straining against their leashes as the troops struggled up the incline.

Dane spotted Sanchez in the lead. He put the HK to his shoulder. "Let 'em have it."

He and Nina opened up with single shots, the SMGs popping in a one-two rhythm. Dane missed Sanchez, the incline throwing off his aim, and Sanchez dropped, shouting orders as two of his troops fell with hits to the chest.

Two loose dogs, in furious mode, charged the tree stump. Dane fired once, missed. Nina's shot stopped one of the animals, while the other zeroed in. Dane fired again and hit the dog, who stopped a few feet from the stump. His nose pointed right at Dane and Nina's hiding spot.

Dane fired again, shifting his aim with each pull of the trigger. Nina's gun chattered while Dane pitched one of the grenades from his web belt. He leaped out of the stump and covered Nina while she followed. They ran into the thick.

The grenade exploded and somebody screamed.

Leaves smacked at them as they ran. The incline started to level. They found a hiding spot and dropped flat with about fifteen meters between them.

Staring through the thick of the jungle was like looking into heavy fog. Dane listened for sounds. Boots, voices, knocking of loose equipment. He heard Sanchez giving orders. His people were splitting up into groups. Rustling ahead. Dane triggered a burst and saw a man fall back, but another took his place. Dane rolled as automatic fire came his way, the rounds slicing through the foliage.

Nina lined up her sights and fired as the shooter dropped out of sight.

Dane changed magazines. Shots popped around him as Sanchez and the troops fired blindly. Dane jumped as each round whistled past him.

Nina threw another grenade. She took off running and Dane followed. The explosion shook the ground but missed targets. The troopers rose to fire. The rounds nicked foliage around Dane and Nina. They found a log and rolled over it, staying flat on the other side.

"How's your ammo?" he said.

"One mag left."

"Same here. One grenade, too."

They popped over the top of the log to fire at targets. Screams, running, Sanchez shouting. A grenade sailed overhead, bounced off a tree and detonated behind them.

Dane saw the trooper who had tossed the bomb and shot him in the face. He reloaded. Both he and Nina ceased fire for a moment. Dane plucked his last grenade and gestured for Nina to give him her last, which she did. Dane pulled one pin and tossed one away. He threw the second in the opposite direction. The first blast made the troops scatter, and they ran into the second, multiple screams carried with the thunder of the explosion.

Dane readied his HK once again.

Rustling behind them. Dane and Nina whirled as Sanchez broke through the leaves with his automatic rifle poised to fire.

A shot cracked. The top of Sanchez's head vanished in a spray of chunky red. He collapsed.

More leaves rustled as another trooper in camo joined Dane and Nina, smoke trickling from the muzzle of his M-16.

Dane said, "Here's our midget."

"Little person, dear." To the boy Nina said, "Who are you?"

"I am Paco Gomez. My father leads the rebels against the Gringo Dragon and El Presidente."

"How about that?" Dane said, with a glance at Nina. To the boy, "Will you take us to your father?"

The boy started to answer but Nina interrupted.

"Steve," Nina said. She found a two-way radio on Sanchez's belt. Dane took it from her. He pressed the Talk button.

"Anybody home?"

Lassen's voice responded. "We're almost there, Sanchez, just hold a little longer."

"Oh, sorry, Cyrus, Sanchez is flat on the ground. He's buzzard bait. He's kaput. He's got a hole in his head for his brains to leak out. In other words, he's dead. And you're next."

As Lassen replied, Dane turned off the two-way.

"Where to, kid?"

"Not kid. I'm Paco. This way!"

The young solider led them away at a quick pace.

"Why you not thank me for rescuing you?" Paco said.

"We didn't need to be rescued," Dane said.

"Stephen!"

"But that was good shooting, kid."

"I told you I'm not a kid!"

Chapter Thirty-Four

They walked steadily, at a brisk pace, following the young soldier.

"Why are you out here alone, Paco?" Dane said.

"I look for my Uncle Rico. He and two others come out here to kill the Dragon, but they didn't come back."

"Stop."

The boy stopped and turned.

Dane fished the dog tags from his pocket.

"We found your uncle, son. I'm sorry."

He put the dog tags in the boy's left hand. Paco examined the ID plate sadly.

"My uncle was a good warrior," he said. He put the tags around his neck. "We will avenge him."

The reaction stunned Dane. Of all the horror and trauma he'd experienced in combat over the years, to watch a 12-year-old boy react in such a fashion hit him hard. But he shouldn't have been surprised. When evil grips your world, you become immune to its abuse.

Paco had seen a lot of violence in his young life.

Dane wouldn't rest until the kid saw no more.

"Stay behind me," the boy said. "Not much further

to go."

They marched.

Paco had no trouble with the higher obstacles that Dane and Nina had to dodge. Presently he stopped and reached into a patch of ground. He lifted a lid and revealed a tunnel opening. He slithered down and beckoned Dane and Nina to follow. They dropped through the opening, Nina pulling the lid shut behind her.

Candles resting in dugouts along the wall lit the way. Dane and Nina needed to crawl, while Paco only hunched. He looked back periodically, leading them through the winding tunnel.

"Where are we going?" Dane said.

"Camp. I help you, maybe you help us. Nobody's ever come out of the Gringo Dragon's palace before."

Dane grinned at Lassen's nickname.

"We use these tunnels to ambush El Presidente's forces," Paco said. "Sometimes they find them, but we always dig new ones."

"Pretty handy," Dane said.

Some of the candles they passed had gone out, throwing sections of the tunnel into total darkness. But Dane and Nina forged ahead until lit candles returned.

"Did you light these?" Dane said.

"On my way today, yes," Paco said.

The boy stopped at a ladder and climbed to another hatch, which he pushed open. He started talking as he went up through the hatch, and when Dane stuck his head through, the reason why awaited. Four armed men trained M-16s on him. Dane stepped up onto solid ground. One of them yanked away his weapon; another slammed the butt of his rifle into Dane's stomach. Breath left him as he fell onto the ground.

Nina cursed as the troops took her gear and shoved her down beside Dane.

"This is better?" she said.

Paco yelled at the troops in Spanish, repeating the same words, pushing and shoving at the adult soldiers, but they argued back at him and he continued raising his voice in frustration.

A new voice broke in, one deeper and louder and possessing enough authority to silence the troopers. Paco rushed to the new arrival and spoke again, quickly, pulling his uncle's dog tag from his neck to show the man.

His father, Dane surmised. The elder Gomez snapped an order. Guards sharply lifted Dane and Nina to their feet. The soldiers marched them forward. Paco and his father trailed beside them. Paco continued telling his story.

It was a rebel camp like many others, hidden deep in the jungle, full of tents set up in as disciplined a fashion as possible, in this case neatly lined up on two sides with the larger, main tent at the end. Every man and woman carried a weapon. Paco appeared to be the only child. Nina gestured to where camouflaged vehicles sat, just beyond the left row of tents.

Paco's father was tall and trim with short, dark hair, olive skin, dark eyes. Much like Paco. The resemblance was uncanny. Dane supposed he'd looked a lot like his own father as well at that age, but he couldn't remember anymore.

Paco's father showed Dane and Nina into his tent, where Paco pulled some folding chairs out of a corner. Dane and Nina sat across from the older Gomez. He told Paco to scoot and lit a cigarette.

The elder Gomez regarded Dane and Nina through a stream of cigarette smoke. He had acne scars on his left cheek.

"My name is Roberto Gomez, and I am the commander of this group."

"The whole force?" Dane said.

"This camp. I'm a major. My son told me how he found you. Thank you for finding my brother's body."

Major Gomez sat with a straight back, but Dane saw a wariness in his eyes.

"What can we add to the story to convince you we're on your side?" Dane said.

"Why does Lassen want to kill you?"

Dane took a few minutes to explain, leaving out nothing, and Gomez lit another cigarette halfway through the tale. Dane added at the end: "Lassen and Royce are out to turn this country into a criminal sanctuary. The only thing standing in their way is your organization. And Nina and me. Let us help you end this."

"How? What do you bring to us?"

"We know the way in and out of Lassen's palace. He's a major cog. He's the money man in charge of weapons. You can take out President Marco, but Lassen will replace him. You need a coordinated strike to take out them both."

"That's a good idea."

"But?"

"Government troops attacked one of our camps last week. We kept a lot of our weapons and supplies at that camp," Gomez said. "We had a plan to hijack the next shipment of guns coming from the US. They travel down the Pan-American Highway. But those shipments have stopped."

"We blew up the last load," Dane said.

"You mean I blew up the last load," Nina said.

"She did."

Major Gomez said nothing.

"Did they destroy the weapons or take them?" Dane said.

"Little bit of both. What was left was taken to a depot near the airport to replace guns and weapons we blew up recently. We thought if we could cut off the supply of weapons, it might hurt the army. That strategy has not proved useful."

"Then we need to strike there. Take as much as we can. From that point, take advantage of whatever intel you have and hit the capitol, along with the airport and broadcast facilities."

"You're familiar with coups?"

"We call it 'regime change' is the United States," Dane said. "We've been paid to knock over a country or two. This time we work for free."

Gomez ground out his cigarette in the dirt. "I have to talk to my squad leaders." He called for Paco. The boy eagerly rushed over. Gomez told him to find a spare tent and uniforms for Dane and Nina. He added, "We have showers, but they aren't much. Paco will show you."

"Come on," Paco said.

Dane and Nina followed the boy. As he walked, Paco kept adjusting the strap of his M-16 because it constantly slid off his shoulder.

He shouldn't have that gun, Dane thought. He should be kicking a soccer ball and go home at the end of every day.

This is madness.

Chapter Thirty-Five

The showers offered only cold water, stored in a tank, but it still felt good. Dane and Nina cleaned up and donned the uniforms Paco presented. The clothes fit better than the ones Lassen had given them.

The uniform T-shirt was short-sleeved, however, and Paco took an interest in Dane's right arm.

"Did that happen in a fire?" the boy said.

"Yes."

"How?"

"Back when you were maybe five years old, the Gringo Dragon wanted me dead. I was snooping where he didn't want me. His men sabotaged a helicopter I was on, and this happened in the crash."

"How come it's taken years to get back at him?"

"That's a long story."

Paco started to respond when Nina, in uniform, stepped out of the shower and handed her dirty clothes to Dane. He bundled hers and his together. "Can we burn these somewhere?"

Paco nodded.

Nina tied back her wet hair.

"I'll show you your tent," Paco said.

Four rebel troops quickly provided a spare tent, and Paco helped Nina string up the top of the tent while Dane hammered spikes into each corner, the sharp metal-to-metal pounding echoing a short distance.

"Where are you from?" Paco said to Nina.

"Russia."

"Why did you leave?"

"I wanted to see the world."

"I've never been out of San Remo," Paco said.

"Where would you like to go?"

"Where else is there to go?"

Dane pounded home the final spike, and Nina and Paco tightened the tent's support rope to a pair of trees on either side.

The war council continued in Gomez's tent. Other troops went about their business. Only Paco acknowledged Dane and Nina.

Nina said, "How long have you been fighting?"

Paco counted on his fingers. "Four years. I hid with my mother until she died. Then I joined Papa."

"What happened to her?"

"She got sick and we didn't have a doctor." Paco picked up his rifle from the tree and slung it over his shoulder. "Dinner's not for a while, but I can get you a little food if you want."

"Sure," Dane said.

Paco ran off.

Dane moved behind Nina and rubbed her shoulders. Her muscles relaxed and she let out a low moan.

"Poor kid," she said.

"We've seen it a hundred times."

"It's sad that we get used to it. The world shouldn't be like this."

"The only way to end it is to not have any people at all. I'm not sure that's the answer, either."

Paco returned with a steaming metal cup in each hand. He handed them to Dane and Nina.

"Tortilla soup," he said. He pulled mashed pieces of bread from his uniform blouse. Dane and Nina each took a piece.

"Be right back." Paco ran off again.

Dane and Nina sat in front of the tent and dipped the bread into the soup.

"Lassen said this group is unorganized," Nina said.

"I remember."

"Is that your impression?"

"I haven't seen them fight. I don't know."

"If they've been fighting for four years, you'd think they'd have made some progress," Nina said.

"This stuff takes time. They need to seed the cities with fighters, have everybody in place and standing by for orders. Maybe now with the Gomez brother dead, they'll be motivated."

"Maybe because we here, they're motivated."

"Sometimes you need a fire lit under your ass, yeah," Dane said.

After a full dinner of more soup with beans and chorizo, Major Gomez joined Dane and Nina at their tent. They sat on the ground. Paco wanted to stay for the conversation, and his father said okay. The boy sat quietly while his father did the talking.

"This war started when Marco killed my father,"

Gomez said. "My father was a teacher and a writer. A man of peace. He thought change could be achieved through peaceful means. My brother and I told him he was wrong."

"What's been happening these last four years, Major?" Dane said.

"A lot of waste. I'm not sure we're ready for this strike you're suggesting."

"You have to have a rough plan," Dane said. "Explain that to me."

"In the cities is where we'll start. My assassins wait in the cities. Marco has representatives in every urban area, carrying out his orders. They control the army in those regions. With them gone, the troops will be running around without leadership."

"Sounds strong," Dane said. "I agree with it."

The major stared at the ground.

"After that?" Dane prompted.

"We hit the presidential palace and other areas of importance."

"It's now or never, Major," Dane said. "It sounds like you have a plan, but you're afraid."

"My father was a man of peace. I want to avenge him. I struggle with whether or not he would agree with me."

"A father's influence is hard to break."

"My son," Gomez said. "He'll never be the same after this."

"You're right. War changes you. You can't go back to what you were, but you can adapt to who you will be when the fighting is over. Your son will be a better man than either you or your father, I promise."

Gomez didn't reply.

"You've never fought a war before, have you?" Dane

said.

Gomez shook his head. "All we know about fighting, we had to learn the hard way."

"And now it's time to put that knowledge to work. If not now, Marco and Lassen and their friends will have an iron grip on this country that you'll never be able to break. Paco will end up like your brother. You, too, probably."

Gomez nodded. "I agree."

"What have your people told you?"

"They say they are ready," Gomez said. "We'll hit the depot while other teams start their own campaign, which includes a series of assassinations. After that, I figured you would want to revisit Lassen's property."

"For sure." Dane said.

Paco said, "Can I go?"

"No, you stay here."

"But, Papa—"

"I need you here, Paco. If we do not succeed, you need to escape with the rest."

"You won't fail."

"From your lips to God's ears."

"So, I can go?"

"No."

"Papa—"

"This discussion is over, Paco."

Paco let out a sharp breath and glowered at the ground.

"We'll need some weapons, Major," Dane said.

"We had an argument about you two," Major Gomez said, lighting a cigarette. "Some of my men don't trust you."

"We've been here long enough that if we had government troops behind us, they'd be here already. You'd all have been wiped out."

Major Gomez rose. "I know. Paco, get them some weapons."

Paco kept his mouth shut and departed.

"He's good in a fight," Dane said. "Saved our lives."

"I know."

Major Gomez walked away.

Nina turned to Dane. "That was some nice psycho-analyzing you did, Steve."

"I'm full of surprises, aren't I?"

"I hope you're right about them."

Dane's face remained stoic. "Me too."

Chapter Thirty-Six

Paco pushed a handcart over to Dane and Nina. On the cart were a pair of beat-up M-16s and pistol belts containing Beretta 9-millimeter 92F auto-loaders.

"They work, but they're old," Paco said. "Need help with them?"

Dane lifted one of the M-16s and faked a frown. He knew the weapon backward and forward from his Marine days. He said, "It's been a while. Why don't you show us?"

"All I know is the AK-47," Nina said.

Paco leaned the rifle against the cart and gave a lesson on how to work the M-16, from loading to shooting and aiming. He had Dane and Nina demonstrate back to him and beamed with delight when they did everything he showed them correctly. He then helped them stuff cartridges into magazines.

Major Gomez came over and inspected their gear, nodding in approval.

"Our depot strike team goes out tonight," the major said. "But not from here. Headquarters changed the assignment. We're to study the presidential retreat and wait for a delivery."

"Is it Christmas already?" Nina said.

"They have mortar tubes at the arms depot, and I requested a few of them."

"That'll help," Dane said. "If you have pictures of the retreat, we can go over what we know."

"Follow me," Major Gomez said.

Dane and Nina joined Gomez in the main tent, where the major and his team leaders set out photos and a hand-drawn map of the presidential retreat.

The meeting continued, with Dane offering strategy suggestions. When a lieutenant brought in a radio and set it up on another table, Gomez ended the meeting and they listened to the strike team hitting the arms depot.

The chatter was all in Spanish. Paco came up to Dane's left and translated for him and Nina.

"They're in two groups, cutting through the perimeter fence."

More chatter.

"First group is through."

A burst of excited radio traffic blasted through the speaker. Gunfire crackled in the background.

"Second group's been discovered," Paco said.

The speaker fell silent. Gomez and his team leaders stared intently at the radio. Gomez flicked his lighter with shaky fingers.

Dane let out a sigh. If the first strike force could take advantage of the second group's discovery, the first could hit the depot while the government troops were diverted. But the cost in lives would be high.

That was always the trade-off, no matter the conflict. If they lost too many, the strike team would have to withdraw. Mission failed. If they somehow broke through, only half the force would accomplish the goal. Some was better than none, but if the rebels were as hard up as Gomez let on, "some" would hardly give them the required tools.

More hurried chatter crackled over the speaker.

"They're in," Paco said.

Dane nodded.

Major Gomez finally lit a cigarette. Nina waved away a cloud of smoke that drifted her way.

A group of rebel troops gathered around the front of the tent, all of them silent. Only the rusting trees made any sound.

The silence lasted for what seemed like forever. Nobody moved.

Eventually a male voice echoed over the speaker and the rebels cheered.

"They did it!" Paco said. "They're loading the trucks now!"

Dane stepped away and walked beyond the perimeter of the camp with the M-16 in hand. Okay. Now the team had to make their deliveries. Like Santa Claus.

After that, the final battle would commence.

He tapped the trigger of the M-16. He wanted Lassen. He wanted Royce—but there had been no sign of Royce at the palace. Had he been hiding? Or was he somewhere else?

Dane felt more energized than ever. Even if he perished in the fight, the enemy had to fall.

That was all that mattered.

Leaves crunched behind Dane and he turned. Paco stopped mid-step. Dane gestured for him to come closer.

"Do you get scared before a fight?" Paco said.

"Always."

"Why do you fight?"

"Because there are people who can't fight for themselves," Dane said.

Paco nodded. "I'm fighting so kids like me can play football whenever they want, and so we have doctors for when somebody else's mother is sick."

Dane looked into the distance. Paco was too young to be thinking things like that. He said, "Don't be mad at your father."

"But I want to be there."

"This fight isn't as important as the next one. You won't need a gun but it's just as intense."

"What do you mean?"

"When you get rid of El Presidente, you're going to need a new government. The new government will need new leaders. You can be one of those leaders, Paco."

The boy blinked a few times.

"Your father wants to make sure you get to do that."

"What if I'm not smart enough?"

"Paco, if you can sneak over to spy on the Gringo Dragon, you're smart enough, trust me."

"I'd rather be a soldier."

Dane smiled. "Tell me that again when every joint in your body hurts."

"That won't be for a while yet," the boy said.

Dane stifled a laugh.

"Am I interrupting?" Nina said as she approached.

"Just guy talk," Dane said.

"The strike team got the mortar launchers," she said. "They'll be here in a few hours. We move out at dawn."

"Finally," Dane said.

Cyrus Lassen paced on one of the presidential retreat's upper balconies. He wore a clean white suit and a scowl as he spoke into a phone with Perry Royce on the other end. Lassen updated Royce on the rebel strike. The sky steadily darkened, the jungle beyond the property melting into the night.

"Did they get everything?" Royce said.

"They got enough."

"Dane is with them?"

"I'm positive. Same as I'm sure that he was intercepted by a rebel patrol. They're coming back. The rebels will hit the capitol, and Dane will lead the charge here."

"Taking you out won't stop anything," Royce said.

"Dane will have his revenge."

"Or you will."

"Indeed. But if I fall, Perry—"

"I will hunt Dane to the ends of the earth, and this time I won't stop for anything."

"He'll turn every western intelligence agency against you," Lassen said. "You'll have nowhere to hide."

"I have a few tricks up my sleeve, Cyrus. Don't count me out just yet. But make sure you stop Dane in San Remo. Otherwise everything we've accomplished to this point gets wiped out."

"I am as motivated as you, Perry."

Lassen ended the call. He stepped up to the railing and looked down at the grounds. His wife should have been there with him. They were supposed to have had many more years together. Steve Dane took that away from him. Lassen's face took a grim set. Now he'd take Dane's life away from him.

Let them try and beat me!

Chapter Thirty-Seven

When the strike team contingent arrived with a trio of mortar launchers and a supply of rockets, Major Gomez rallied the troops for a final briefing. They would be part of a simultaneous push against the capitol. Rebel agents in the city were already targeting El Presidente's associates using car bombs and bullets. The presidential palace, the TV and radio station, and the airport also had a force assigned to take those targets down.

He showed the group a map of the Gringo Dragon's retreat and divided up his people into four teams. They'd hit on all sides and rally in the front courtyard.

Finally, Major Gomez ordered everyone to prepare their gear and get ready for inspection.

With barely any light to see by, Dane and Nina packed the last of their gear by feel. They stepped out of the tent to find Paco waiting.

"Don't get hurt," the boy said.

"We'll be back," Dane said.

"Not here. We're moving as soon as you leave."

Major Gomez called the raiding party to the center of the camp for the promised inspection. Presently they marched into the jungle. Dane waved at Paco before disappearing into the foliage. The boy's eyes never left him.

Dane and Nina broke off from the group and found a rise overlook-ing part of the retreat wall. Once the mortar shells started to fall, they'd advance. The major's soldiers would follow shortly thereafter.

Dane's focus was the patio doors across the grass from the wall. No front door for him.

It wasn't a long wait. When the mortars began sailing overhead, they made a momentary whoosh before exploding on the ground inside the walls of the Gringo Dragon's lair. Lassen's troops scattered for cover, the randomly aimed bombs dropping mere feet from where they sought that cover, blasting the walls of the mansion, with debris filling the air and creating more hazards. The blasts shook the ground, smoke rising in the compound, held in by the wall but drifting skyward.

Dane and Nina lay flat about twenty yards from the wall, watching the smoke, hearing the screaming. The mortar barrage would end with the last shell blasting a hole in the wall for Dane and Nina to run through. The wait was excruciating. An anxious Dane breathed deeply, wiping his sweaty right hand on the seat of his camo pants before grabbing the grip of the M-16 once again.

The bombardment ceased, the crackle of automatic weapons and the shouts from onrushing troops replacing the explosive cacophony.

"Did they forget?" Nina said.

Dane rolled onto his side to scan the sky.

Then the whoosh came once again. Dane shouted, "Incoming!" and rolled on top of Nina. The blast hit with the force of a thousand hammers. Dirt and concrete debris pelted the ground around them, and when Dane looked up through the dust and smoke, an entire section of the wall had been reduced to chunky rubble.

The dust drifted over them and they coughed, then Dane and Nina clutched their weapons close and charged into the fray, climbing over the debris to step onto the palace grounds as men fought and died all around them.

Rebel forces moved in from the main entrance and another hole in the western side of the property. Dane and Nina dropped low and crawled to a hedgerow.

"This is lousy cover," Nina said.

Bullets whistled overhead, snapping through the top of the hedge, whining off the wall behind them.

"This isn't cover at all," Dane said.

Presidential troops fired from positions on the ground, but the rebel advance faced the worst resistance from the balconies of the palace, where troops used the low walls for cover and fired down at the rebel troops. The rebels were focused on the front and the western side. The eastern walls Dane and Nina had come through did not present a major threat. They may have thought a stray shell had hit the wall, nothing more, Dane thought. He examined the length of wall to their right.

"What's the plan?" Nina said.

"Stay low along the wall and hit the side of the house. Through that patio to the French windows."

"It's getting hot here; let's go."

Dane moved out through the smoke with Nina behind him, the ground near the wall slightly slanted, making a steady advance difficult. Two presidential troopers exited the French doors at the patio. One carried a Kalashnikov rifle, while the other cradled a shoulder-fired rocket launcher in his arms, with three more strapped across his back.

"Take 'em!" Dane shouted, dropping and rolling away from the wall. He targeted the trooper with the AK. The M-16 bucked against his shoulder; the trooper tried to bring his weapon up but wasn't fast enough. The M-16's tumbling bullets tore into the trooper's midsection. The man fell forward, his partner not far behind as Nina's rounds blew one knee apart. Both men tumbled to the ground, the second losing the cradled rocket launcher. As he tried to move, Dane fired again, sending a round straight through the man's head.

"Hurry!" Dane said. He ran to the dead man with the rocket launchers, slinging one across his back, taking another in his left hand while gripping the M-16 in his right.

"Get down!" Nina shouted, shoving Dane with a foot while she snapped up her rifle, looking for a target along the wall.

Dane followed her gaze. "I don't see anybody."

"I could have sworn there was somebody." Nina lowered her rifle.

Dane rose. He slung the second rocket launcher, both making an X across his back. He and Nina crossed the patio, slipping inside via the open French doors. The side room they stood in was quiet. All of the balcony shooting and commotion came from above them.

Dane took the lead and advanced up a small set of stairs to a raised floor of the rest of the room. He stopped at a corner. Ahead of them lay the front of the house. The hinges held up the shattered front door. A line of windows stretched across the front on either side of the door. Bullets had popped holes in the glass.

The walls and floor shook from the thunder of gunfire above. Nina started to speak but Dane didn't hear. He moved into the front hall and followed the windows to the left of the door. He stayed low. The window farthest to the left had the most damage, a couple of large holes, and Dane peeked through them. The bottom edge of the second-floor balcony was clearly visible.

He could use the support columns out front for cover and blast the balcony with a rocket.

And then what? Have the works crash down on him?

Stupid idea.

Dane left the window, waved Nina on from the corner where she'd remained, and started for a staircase. As his feet hit the first step, Nina stopped and covered the landing above, her finger barely touching the trigger.

Dane made the first landing and halted. The staircase continued off to their left. Ahead, a wide hallway with rooms on either side and the wide balcony at the end.

"As soon as you fire, the shooters upstairs are coming down," Nina said.

"Then you'd better be ready for them."

Dane readied one of the rocket launchers, extending the tube, which released the aiming sight. He put the tube to his shoulder. The fighters on the balcony—he counted five—shuffled positions as they continued to exchange fire with rebel troops.

He aimed at the floor of the balcony and loosed the missile. The projectile flashed from the tube, the exhaust trail stinging Dane's eyes as he and Nina dropped flat.

The blast filled the room, debris flying like a swarm of angry bees. Dane looked through the smoke. What remained of the balcony was a jagged line, most of it having fallen below to the front steps in a massive pile of debris and bodies.

Dane dropped his head to the floor to suck air. Nina coughed.

"We gotta move back!" she said.

Dane shoved her toward the stairs, and they hustled down, gasping, coughing. They stopped in the middle of the staircase and leaned against the wall.

When the swarm of uniformed troops crashed through the front of the house, Dane shoved Nina back and raised the M-16.

"Steve, wait!"

Dane lowered the rifle as Major Gomez emerged at the head of the group.

"You're all right?" the major said, approaching the stairs.

Dane and Nina acknowledged their wellness.

"When you blasted the balcony, we moved close and got the shooters on the third level."

"Do we control the property?"

"All except for—"

"Lassen. Any sign of him escaping?"

"The grounds are sealed off, so unless he has a secret tunnel—"

"Right. Stay here, Nina."

"Steve—"

"Stay!" Dane started up the stairs, slapping a new magazine into the M-16.

Chapter Thirty-Eight

The smoke and dust on the second floor made his eyes hurt, but Dane powered through, covering his mouth with his left arm, the M-16 out in front. He made it through the smoke and up to the third floor and its long hallway, with the polished tiled floor. Rooms on either side, double doors at the end. Dane started forward, his free hand on the M-16's forward handguards, the stock burrowed into his shoulder. The double doors grew larger as he neared. Lassen could be elsewhere, but the big room was Dane's first choice. It offered enough space for a final battle. He didn't think Lassen would run. They both wanted to kill each other, and running didn't figure into either of their plans.

Dane reached the tall double doors and pushed one open, the snout of the M-16 leading the way.

Cyrus Lassen sprang from his hiding spot along the wall and let out a yell as he brought a long sword down from above his head. The blade crashed against the M-16. Dane grunted as the weapon left his hands, the impact sending a sharp sting through his fingers, up the length of each arm.

Lassen raised the sword again as Dane reached for the

holstered Beretta 9-millimeter, but as the blade whistled down, he dove to the right instead.

The big dining room with the table dead center indeed offered room to fight, but little cover. The chairs around the table would not stop an assault from that blade for long.

Dane dug the 9-millimeter from the holster as Lassen closed the gap between them and raised the sword like a baseball bat. His eyes showed a fury Dane had never seen. Dane's finger tightened on the Beretta as the sword arced down and Dane pulled the gun back. The blade was going for his wrist. The edge struck the gun instead, shearing off the first two inches of the barrel and reducing the gun to a useless hunk of steel.

Dane threw the gun. Lassen easily dodged, and the steel clattered on the floor and slid into a corner.

Lassen moved forward, breathing hard. Dane moved back, putting the table between him and Lassen.

"No more weapons," Lassen said, "so you retreat like a coward."

"More like a quick moment to evaluate the battlefield."

Lassen took two quick steps forward, Dane shuffling back toward the doors where the M-16 had fallen. Unlike the pistol, it had not been terribly damaged. The hand-guards were broken, but the rifle might still fire.

"Always the joker."

"I learned from the best."

"And who might that be?"

"A certain bloke from England."

Dane grabbed a chair and shoved. The brightly polished floor provided an excellent surface for the chair to slide. As Lassen stepped aside, Dane dove for the M-16, skidding across the tile on his stomach.

Dane's hands grasped the rifle. The handle on top and

the front sight were smashed. He rolled onto his back. Lassen raised the sword. Dane's finger found the trigger, and flame licked from the muzzle, the flash obliterating the person before him. Lassen fell back, the sword landing with a clang, Lassen's body following.

Dane, gasping, tossed the M-16 aside and scrambled on hands and knees for the sword. He gained his feet and pivoted to the fallen Gringo Dragon.

Lassen lay flat, his fiery eyes fixed on the ceiling, his guts splattered all over the floor. Somehow, he still breathed, albeit slowly.

Dane, breathless, sweating, the sword held aloft, stared at the dying man. There was still one more piece to the puzzle—Royce—and Lassen was in no condition to provide clues.

Lassen turned his head to Dane. His mouth remained open, but the lips did not move. His eyes studied Dane one last time.

Dane swung the sword down, separating the dragon's head from its body.

Dane stepped outside into the warm air.

The aftermath of the battle was the same he'd seen all over the world, the unwounded helping the wounded and creating a place for the dead. A handful of troops stood ready by the opening in the wall. Dane looked up at the mansion. More rebel troops kept watch from elevated positions.

"Nice sword."

Dane turned. Nina and Major Gomez stopped behind him.

"I slew a dragon with it," Dane said, and stabbed the point into the earth. It stuck out of the ground like a crusade grave marker. Dane said to Gomez, "What's our status, Major?"

"We have reinforcements coming from the camp. I had to send some men to the capitol. We took the presidential palace, and President Marco was killed trying to escape in a car. There is still hard-liner resistance."

"How does that feel?"

"I wish I had killed him myself."

Dane understood, but couldn't put it into words. He and the major shared a bond in wanting to avenge their fathers' deaths. Eventually, he hoped Gomez found satisfaction in the victory.

"Nina and I remain at your service if you want."

Nina said, "We talked about that. He doesn't want."

"Don't take it the wrong way," Major Gomez said. "When everything is done—"

"I get it, Major. You don't want anybody saying you had help."

"You provided a great deal. Maybe even the push we needed to end this."

"And you pulled us out of a nasty spot in the jungle. May we see Paco one more time?"

"He's on his way with the reinforcements."

Dane and Nina sat on the front steps and watched the continuing cleanup.

"You were right after all," Nina said.

"I bet that hurt to say."

She nuzzled him. "No, it didn't."

A moment of silence passed between them.

"How do we get out of here?" Nina said, her head on Dane's shoulder, his right arm around her.

"I'm sure there's a working phone somewhere within

fifty miles," Dane said. "Len can send a jet. If not, we have plenty of friends we can call."

"Do you think they can hold the country?"

"Yes."

"Really?"

"I hope so."

"What about Royce?"

"He wasn't here. That means he's somewhere else."

She jabbed him in the belly. "I could have said that."

Dane laughed. "It means Lassen's reach is further than the US or this place. We have a few more cages to rattle."

"What if he's gone underground?"

"Doesn't matter. I'll never stop looking now that I know who I'm looking for."

She patted Dane's leg. "We will never stop."

"That's what I meant."

Chapter Thirty-Nine

Dane borrowed a cigar from a rebel sergeant who had brought them to celebrate a victory and put a match to the tip. The bodies of dead rebels had been placed near the eastern wall and covered with tarps. The dead presidential troops were piled on the far side of the mansion. Buzzards circled overhead waiting for their opportunity to peck at the flesh.

Other rebels were looting the house, emerging with food and liquor and other items of value.

Typical war zone. They never changed.

Major Gomez came over again.

"We secured the radio and television station," he said. "We're broadcasting news of the coup."

Dane blew smoke. The cigar had no band and he couldn't tell the make by taste, but it had a rich flavor. "Good. That's huge."

Troops started shouting. A tracked vehicle rolled through the front, more armed rebels jumping out and joining the rest of the force. One small soldier broke from the group and ran across the field to jump into his father's arms.

"You're all right!" Paco said.

The boy broke from his father and hugged Dane next.

"Did we win?" Paco said, looking between the two.

"We won, Paco," the major said, but Dane noted a weariness in the man's voice, indicating he knew that a totally different fight loomed over the horizon.

The Jeep bounced along the rough road, winding through a town toward the airport. Dane up front with Major Gomez behind the wheel, Nina and Paco in the back. Paco held his M-16 between his knees.

Too much debris slowed their progress through some of the streets. There had been heavy fighting everywhere, and a mix of rebel soldiers and eager civilians was hustling to clear the mess.

Troops saluted as Gomez drove by; people cheered. Some of them, anyway. Others wore blank stares of the walking wounded. The coup had affected everybody, somehow. It wasn't time to celebrate yet. If ever.

Dane tried not to think about anything he saw, but it affected him nonetheless. The people were free to determine their own destiny now, but the cost had been high. The recovery would take longer than the war.

Once beyond the town limits, Gomez increased speed. Lush greenery sat on either side of the two-lane road.

A finger tapped Dane's arms. He turned.

Paco leaned forward. "I wish you didn't have to go."

Dane studied Paco's brown eyes. There was still some innocence in them. He looked nothing like the people they had just passed.

"Make me a promise, Paco."

"What?"

"As soon as we're gone, trade that rifle for a football."

The boy sat back, a little confused. Nina smiled and patted his leg.

Dane had indeed found a working phone at Lassen's and contacted Lukavina, who was glad to hear from him and eager for the update on San Remo. Dane promised to tell him everything after they landed in the States, but that meant Len had to send a plane.

The CIA Cessna Citation waited on the tarmac as Gomez drove through the gate checkpoint. The property was crawling with rebel troops at various posts.

Gomez stopped the Jeep beside the jet. The four of them exited the Jeep. Paco left his rifle. He hugged Nina first, then went to Dane and hugged him. Dane let out a laugh.

"Nobody will ever say they don't know how you feel, Paco."

"He takes after his mother," the major said.

Paco stepped back, and Dane and the major shook hands.

"Thank you."

"My pleasure, Major."

Gomez smiled and bowed slightly toward Nina. "Take care, señora."

"I hope you build a wonderful country."

Gomez answered only with a weak smile.

Dane took her hand and they climbed the steps to the jet. A CIA man in a dark suit waited at the top and introduced himself as Dan Reese. "I have new clothes for you and the shower's in back."

"Me first," Nina said, and brushed past both men.

Dane turned for one last wave. The Gomez father and son waved back. Dane stepped deeper into the plane and Reese pulled the door shut.

The circular shower was narrow and hard to move in, with only a thin curtain to keep the splashing contained, but Dane felt like a new man when he turned off the water. The clothes provided by Lukavina fit well and he felt relieved to put on a long-sleeved shirt once again. Dane paused as he buttoned the cuffs of the right sleeve. He wondered for the first time if he covered his scars to hide them from others or only from himself. But it wasn't a train of thought he felt like following right now. There were more important things on his mind.

He found Nina seated on a chair with her legs crossed. She rotated the chair to face him, grinning as she held a glass of vodka.

"I'm breaking the fast."

Dane came over and took the glass from her, downed what remained and gave back the glass.

"Me too."

He dropped into the seat next to her.

"What changed your mind?"

"Where's our chaperone?"

"Up with the pilots."

"When Lassen was coming at me with the sword, I saw anger in his eyes that I've never seen before. He didn't just want to get even, he hated me. I wondered if I was like that."

He raised an eyebrow as Nina dropped her eyes to the floor.

"Is that a yes?"

She looked at him. "I've never seen you the way you were when we saw Gallagher. You've shot guys before, but you were always detached. You mentally tortured that man."

"You feel sorry for him?"

"No," she said. "I'm just pointing out the difference. I don't want to see you go over the edge."

"This isn't just another job."

"I think what you're trying to say is that it should be. If only to protect yourself."

"I think you're right. Where'd you get the vodka?"

She nodded toward the galley at the back of the plane. Dane retrieved the bottle and another glass. He filled both. They clinked glasses and drank.

"So now we find Royce?" Nina said.

"Lukavina's already started, but I have a feeling he'll be looking for us, too."

"Why don't we just let him?"

Dane pressed his lips together and thought for a long time.

"I don't think we'll have to wait long," he said.

Chapter Forty

The jet landed in the US ten hours later. Dane and Nina slept most of the way.

At the end of the steps sat two black GM SUVs with tinted windows. Armor fortified each vehicle to repel small- and intermediate-arms fire. They were also fitted with fancy com systems and anti-personnel features, such as tear gas canisters mounted under the chassis. Men in black suits, armed with submachine guns, waited outside the vehicles. The engines of both vehicles were already running.

"Armed escorts?" Nina said.

"I guess we're pretty important," Dane said.

They reached the end of the steps, and the leader of the CIA team opened the back doors of the first SUV. Dane and Nina climbed inside.

The security team communicated over their radios, and the two SUVs set off.

The time passed in mind-numbing but scenic dullness.

Then the first rocket-propelled grenade struck.

The SUVs moved at an accelerated pace, following one of the many winding back roads to CIA headquarters. Off Dane's right, the forest stretched upward for miles. To the left of the vehicles, a steep drop led only to one's doom.

The convoy slowed once the two-lane road narrowed to one.

Dane didn't believe it when he saw it, but there was also no mistake. A puff of smoke off the road, followed by the shriek of a finned, rocket-propelled grenade closing the gap between forest and target.

Dane shouted, "RPG!" as the rocket struck the pavement in front of the SUV. Dane threw his arms in front of his face. The explosion shattered the windshield and filled the cabin with flying shards. Nina screamed. The SUV continued forward, the front end falling into the crater created by the blast. The SUV's sudden jolt sent everybody forward, bodies colliding, automatic weapons fire slamming into the bodywork, but the bulletproofing kept the rounds from destroying the side windows.

The security team in the second SUV lit up the radio.

"Back up, back up!"

Dane shoved the unconscious driver out, crawling over his body to the pavement. He ran to the rear door and helped out another agent, then Nina. The remaining agent in the back was either out cold or dead. Dane reached for his weapon and jacked back the charging handle.

Then the next rocket struck.

The second SUV blew, a tsunami of heat and flame roaring over Dane and the others. Nina grabbed a stray handgun and crouched beside Dane.

"Get back!" she shouted, pulling Dane away from the SUV. They and the security agent raced for the shoulder of the road behind them.

The third RPG lifted the SUV off the ground, the ball of flame engulfing the steel body, the security agent running beside Dane falling as sharp pieces of metal impaled him. Nina stumbled, catching one of Dane's legs as she fell. He hit the pavement hard, breath leaving him. He rolled onto his back. Nina lay flat on the pavement, a growing pool of blood under her face. Then armed men, wearing masks and toting automatic rifles, emerged from the forest.

Dane raised the HK submachine gun and triggered a long burst of .45 slugs. The rounds cut through the leading gunman, stitching the hooded shooter from chest to face. The back of the man's head sprayed blood and bone on the shooter behind him. Dane's next burst put down that second man. The heat from the burning SUVs cut through his clothes and touched the back of his neck. Sweat covered his skin.

Somebody tossed a grenade. It sailed overhead, aimed right for Dane's position. As it reached the top of its arc and started down, Dane rolled. When he reached the opposite edge of the road, he went over the side. The grenade blast shook the ground. Shrapnel rained overhead. Dane kept falling, landing hard on a wooded slope, the wind knocked out of him. His vision spun and he sucked air in short gasps. Every bone in his body hurt, but he focused only on the task before him. Injuries were not the priority.

Dane rose just high enough to bring up his weapon. The masked shooters were spread out on the road. Two of them dragged Nina into the brush. Dane took aim but dropped back as the other shooters saw him and opened fire. Slugs cut through the brush, sharp bits of bark and branches striking his face and neck, the bullets whistling overhead. Dane rose again and returned fire. The hoods retreated into the forest as his salvo reached their last position. He struck none of them. He climbed onto the road and had both feet on the pavement when a fifth RPG shrieked from the forest. The pavement took the hit, and the explosion lifted Dane off his feet and back over the edge of the road.

Dane landed like a ten-ton brick. He lay stunned but forced himself to hands and knees, fighting the searing pain that he now couldn't so easily ignore as the threat of unconsciousness joined the party. His head still spun, and he rose only to find he had no balance. Back on hands and knees, he vomited and rolled onto his side, eyes shut, a low groan escaping his lips.

The enemy was getting away.

And they had Nina.

No cavalry coming to save the day.

How did they know we were coming?

An inside job!

Dane beat back the agony of his injuries and forced himself to stand. The front barrel of the HK had been bent in the fall. Useless. He discarded the weapon and climbed to the pavement. The dead security agent lay on the ground next to his SUV, which burned, the heat intense, almost like a force field Dane couldn't penetrate. He stepped close enough to grab the security agent's ankles and dragged his body away from the vehicle. He took the man's pistol and spare ammo.

And then he charged into the forest.

The hooded gunmen had worn heavy-duty combat boots.

Dane easily followed their sunken steps. He stopped every ten to fifteen yards to examine the tracks. No booby traps to entangle pursuers, he noticed, because they didn't think there were any.

When he heard the distant thump of a helicopter, instinct told him it was not government issue. He powered forward, legs sore from the uphill climb, his lungs burning, the pain biting his insides with more intensity every time he took a step. He kept going. Pain meant he was alive; it felt good to be alive.

Dane passed over the discarded RPG launchers. Still on track. The helicopter sounds grew louder. A burst of sunlight ahead signaled a clearing. Dane ran, leaping over a fallen tree trunk. Then he saw the hooded gunmen. One of them held Nina facedown with a pistol jammed into her neck. Dane braced against a tree and fired twice.

The shots geysered dirt in the clearing. Dane shifted and tried again. Another miss. He hit the dirt as return fire snapped his way. Another grenade bounced off a tree, landing nearby, the explosion a deafening roar. Dane fired from a prone position but there were no more targets. The shooters had taken cover in the foliage.

The chopper dipped into the clearing, a large black passenger helicopter with no visible markings. The hood with Nina shoved her toward the chopper. At least she was moving on her own. The other shooters fired on Dane's position with enough accuracy to hit the tree he lay beside and kick up the dirt around him. He fired a blind shot in return, but all that did was waste ammo.

The covering fire stopped. Dane lifted his head again and saw why.

The last of the hooded gunmen climbed into the helicopter, the pilot lifting off before his passengers had the side door shut. Dane ran into the clearing. He raised the pistol in a two-handed grip, and he fired so fast that the pistol spat lead like a machine gun. The slugs sparked against the fuselage but did no damage. And then the pistol locked open. The chopper flew over the trees and out of sight.

Dane dropped to his knees, gasping; then he fell over and passed out.

He had lost Nina.

Chapter Forty-One

Dane opened his eyes. Len Lukavina looked down at him.

"Where am I?" Dane said. The words croaked from his throat, his mouth cracked and dry.

"Unconscious in a hospital bed and lucky to be alive." Lukavina moved to a chair in the corner and brought it over to the side of the bed. He sat.

"How did you find me?"

"Followed the noise. You're the only one who made it."

"They have Nina."

"We traced the chopper to a local airfield, where they transferred to a pair of vehicles," Lukavina said.

"And split up."

"They changed cars again before we lost them."

Dane started to rise, but his spinning head made him plop right back down. "Oh wow."

"You're not going anywhere. No broken bones, but numerous cuts and abrasions and a doozy of a concussion."

Dane tried to rise again. "They have Nina."

Lukavina put a hand on Dane's chest and pushed him back down. "We've been rattling cages all over the world."

"And you have nothing."

"Not yet."

"How did they know we'd be there, Len?"

Lukavina took a notebook from inside his coat. "Well, this incident did reveal a clue. The only way Royce could have known about your arrival is if he had an inside man. We think we know who that is."

"How?"

"Cell phones are banned in the headquarters building. Before the attack, we recorded an unauthorized cell call followed by the abrupt departure of a man named Andy Swindol. He words in Records."

"Is he running to Royce?"

"He's running somewhere."

"How many eyes on him?"

"As many as we can spare. I thought you might want to call in some help, too."

"No, Len. When I get out of here, I'm going after Royce alone."

"Don't be stupid."

"Excuse me, Len?"

"You need to calm down. Steve, you've done nothing but help others through their problems. Now let others help you."

Dane stared at his friend a moment. He thought about the last expression he saw on Lassen's face, his conversations with Nina. Going in alone would only end one way. His vengeance would be denied.

"Okay," he said. "You're right."

Andy Swindol always knew this day would come.

The Keeper of the Secrets knew The Call would mark the end of his usefulness at headquarters and he'd have no choice but to link up with Royce elsewhere to keep the scheme going.

He made the call. Royce moved assets into position to intercept the convoy…

And per instructions, he was to telephone again for further orders. Get out of the building and head for a rendezvous, where you'll be collected.

Swindol exited the Beltway and drove in heavy surface-street traffic, nervously drumming on the wheel. He wasn't in a car the agency knew. It was his alternate, a getaway car stashed for such an occasion. His other car, with the cell phone the agency undoubtedly now had a lock on sitting in the glove box, was parked in an alley elsewhere in D.C.

He watched street signs closely and didn't notice how heavily he was breathing. The full-blast air conditioner kept the sweat on his face from dripping.

Another block and he turned into a shopping center, the parking lot stuffed and slow-moving shoppers pushing carts and walking too leisurely for his liking. He found a place to park and left the car, pulling at his collar, his custom-fitted suit suddenly feeling like it didn't fit at all. He knew he wasn't losing his mind, but it sure was playing tricks on him.

His feet felt like lead as he crossed the lot to the building, breathing deeply. He now realized just how ill prepared for this day he was. But once he made this next call, all would be okay. Royce would send somebody to fetch him. That was their deal.

He reached the building and went to the pay phone against the wall. The phone sat between the grocery store and a dry cleaner. It was one of several he had mapped out throughout the city. He lifted the receiver and deposited the appropriate amount of change before dialing. Two rings and then a man answered.

"Yes?"

Swindol did not recognize the voice. He said, "It's Swindol, reporting as ordered."

"Wait."

He stifled a curse. Royce could have at least used some hold music.

Swindol turned his back to the phone. People continued to move about, a mother pushing a full shopping cart and trying to control two kids at the same time passing him with little notice. He looked across the parking lot but couldn't see his car. A white SUV was parked near his spot, though. His pulse quickened, but there was no way the FBI could have picked up his trail so quickly. The SUV was but one of many cars in the parking lot. That was all.

As soon as the white SUV stopped near Swindol's car, one man exited the passenger side carrying a small tote.

His left arm was covered with tattoos. He knelt on the passenger side, extracted a rectangular device from the tote and rolled onto his back and under the car. He was there for two minutes before rolling out, grabbing the tote and wiping grimy hands on his jeans. He climbed back into the SUV. The driver put the vehicle in gear and pulled away.

"Swindol?"

The young, now former CIA man, snapped to life, turning away from the parking lot view.

"Good to hear your voice, sir."

"Don't be nervous, you're covered."

A wave of relief washed over Swindol. "What do you want me to do?"

Royce gave instructions, and Swindol repeated them. "See you soon." Royce hung up.

Smiling, Swindol did the same, wiped his face with a handkerchief and walked back to the car. All was well. His feet didn't feel like lead any longer. He unlocked the car and climbed in, noting that the SUV had gone. He thought nothing more about it.

When he turned the ignition key, the car exploded.

Chapter Forty-Two

Dane placed his bare feet on the cold tiled floor and immediately felt dizzy.

He grabbed on to the bed. Lukavina walked in as he rolled back onto the mattress.

"What did I tell you, dummy?"

Dane, breathing hard, only nodded.

"Wherever Nina's at," Lukavina said, stopping bedside, "she's a tough girl. She won't make anything easy."

Dane swallowed. "They don't want her. They want me."

"You need to take it easy, Steve."

"Where's my phone?"

"Someplace you can't get to it."

"Why are you here, Len?"

"Bad news about Swindol. We found bits of him in a blown-up car."

"No surprise."

"That means we're at a dead end."

"Bring me my phone."

"Who are you going to call?" Lukavina said.

"Nobody. I'm going to wait for one."

Nina winced as the truck jolted.

She lay on the floor of the truck, tied at wrists and ankles, and the cold steel beneath her proved quite unforgiving. Worse, she had no idea where she was or where the driver planned to take her. The only thing she knew for sure was that the two gunmen guarding her looked bored, but not unwilling to use their machine pistols should she try anything.

Another bump. Her left shoulder hit hard, and she stifled a cry, shutting her eyes tight. She rolled onto her stomach. Might as well let her chin take a beating for a while. She didn't want to rest on her left side, because the cuts on her head wouldn't appreciate the beating. There was caked blood down the left side of her face, and she wanted a washcloth. Bad.

It was an old truck, the steel floor rusting in spots, a canopy over the bed, a canvas curtain covering the rear. The boots of one of the gunmen were right beside her right ear. If she moved that way even a little, he might think she was coming on to him. He had his face in an iPhone, though. He probably wouldn't notice.

More bouncing. Nina shut her eyes and tried to think of how long they'd been traveling. She'd been woozy from her injuries during the convoy attack, the chopper flight hazier still, but she'd awoken from unconsciousness aboard a passenger jet. Nobody had spoken to her, but they let her know they'd use their guns if necessary. She thought that was a bluff. There was no reason to have her other than as bait for Dane; of course, she didn't need to be alive, they just had to convince him that she was, and he'd come running to her rescue. If he didn't say, "The hell with it," and run off with a blonde in Barbados. She'd have to kick him in the shin for that when she saw him next.

Huh?

She forced thoughts from her head. No sense in going loopy when she needed clarity.

What did she know for sure?

They were on a rough road going somewhere. Destination unknown. She had no shoes and no belt. Taken because they might be used as a weapon. Her bare feet felt dirty; there was grit between her toes. She'd been carried from one point to another with her feet dragging. She didn't remember getting off the plane, so maybe it happened then. Too bad she couldn't analyze said grit and figure out where the soil originated from. She'd have to do everything the old-fashioned way.

Two goons with her, one on his phone, the other she couldn't see. Both armed. Was there a passenger up front with the driver?

She turned her attention to the current environment. The air smelled fresh, minus the occasional putrid exhaust blast. She didn't hear any other vehicles, and they didn't stop for traffic lights.

She sighed with exhaustion. She could spin her thoughts a million miles an hour, and the reality was that she wouldn't have any concrete information until they hefted her out of the truck and to wherever they were taking her. If they'd wanted her dead, she'd have been dead by now.

She rolled onto her right shoulder and bounced some more. Her head hit the steel and she let out a groan. Neither of the gunmen seemed to notice. She glanced at the second gunman, a younger kid with a clean-shaven jaw, who was dozing, the muzzle of his machine pistol lazily drifting with each jolt.

Well. So much for tight security.

The truck rumbled up an incline with the engine struggling, but it was a short climb. As soon as the driver leveled off, the truck stopped, and the engine stopped.

Nina kept quiet as the two gunners rose and tossed the tailgate curtain up over the roof of the canopy. Bright light invaded the space, and Nina squinted her eyes. She rolled onto her back, crunching her abs to pull her upper body up into a sitting position.

The two gunners waited, with a third man standing between them. The third man was in his early 60s and leaned on a cane.

"You must be Royce," she said.

"I am. Get out."

Nina hesitated. The gunners stepped back, raising their machine pistols. Nina scooted forward, grunting with her hands behind her back. She moved forward like a slug, pulling with her legs, scooting her bottom along the truck bed. She stopped with her legs dangling over the tailgate.

"If you expect me to walk, I need my legs free."

Royce gestured to the youngest of the gunners, the one who'd been dozing, who shouldered his weapon long enough to cut the bonds with a knife. He quickly stepped back and pointed his gun at her again. Nina hopped off the tailgate.

"Start walking," Royce said.

"Where?"

"I'm not a patient man, Ms. Talikova."

Nina turned and moved around the side of the truck. Ahead of her sat a single building in a large field of green, with snow-capped mountains far in the distance. A chill bit through her skin. She was in the Alps. The building before her was the only one around with a dirt road running by.

Truly in the middle of nowhere.

Her bare feet actually felt good in the cold grass. She didn't mind that at all. But the rest of her body felt stiff and sore. She bit her lip, trying not to let out any sounds of discomfort. Royce walked beside her, his cane preceding every step, the gunners behind him.

"This is my personal hideaway," Royce said. "You're a privileged guest."

"Why don't you just call me bait?"

Royce laughed. "I suppose we could do that. Whether you're live or dead bait is up to you."

"You know what will happen if I sustain any damage."

"I'm sure. Mr. Dane has become quite a proficient killer. I intend to harm him a great deal."

"Then you'd better kill me, too."

He smiled. "You've yet to meet the lady of the house. You may get your wish."

The front door had a small arch over the top. Royce pushed the door open, the bottom edge scraping against a concrete floor and leading into a wide-open room. A layer of dust covered the floor and the walls. The armed men standing around, six by Nina's quick count, were not dusty at all. Then a woman entered from a side room.

"This is Helden Steuben," Royce said. "She and I are what's left of Lassen's organization."

The woman wore white and was short and stocky, her body thick with muscle—the kind of gal who liked crushing beer cans against her forehead. Nina was a head taller. The woman came forward and grabbed Nina's left arm, almost dragging her across the floor. Nina shuffled to keep up. Royce started issuing orders as Steuben led Nina up a flight of stairs to a narrow hallway, where at the end a ladder stood. The top of the ladder extended through an opening in the ceiling.

"Up," the big woman said.

"In the attic?"

"Up."

"I don't get a—"

The big woman slammed a fist into Nina's belly. A sharp pain filled her body, and Nina gasped for breath, doubling over. The big woman grabbed her shoulder and forced her upright.

"Up!"

Nina gritted her teeth. "My hands are tied, you silly bitch."

The big woman spun Nina around and with one wrench broke the twine locking her wrists together. She twisted Nina's right wrist, bringing her around once again, and pointed at the ladder.

Nina took back her wrist, locking eyes with the woman. Helden Steuben's eyes did not waver. The big woman did not blink.

"I'll kill you later," Nina said.

The big woman let out a grunt.

Nina started climbing, disappearing into the dark attic. Her feet left the last rung and Steuben snatched the ladder away, the trapdoor closing with an abrupt slam, plunging the attic further into darkness.

Nina felt around. At least there was carpet. As her eyes adjusted, she noticed air vents in the wall. Octagonal with the louvers closed. She crossed to one and turned the louvers to the open position, letting in some light and fresh air. Nothing but green hills as far as she could see, and no sign at all of civilization.

She put her back to the wall and sat. No stray noises indicated creepy critters, but maybe they'd appear at night.

She started crawling in a circle, feeling around, tightening the circle with each pass of the open vent. There was nothing in the attic to use as a weapon, no stray items; the place was empty except for her.

She went back to the open vent and sat against the wall once again. The only thing to do was wait for an opportunity to strike. She'd made them free her hands and legs. That was a start. She felt along the edge of the vent flaps, but they were secured tightly to the frame of the vent and made of wood. And not thick wood, either. She might break one free of the frame, but she might as well go after a bull with a fly swatter.

She stretched out and tried to make herself comfortable.

Chapter Forty-Three

"What's the plan?"

Royce sat and placed his cane across his lap. Helden Steuben stood before him with her arms folded. She was a tank of a woman who was all business. He'd never seen her when she wasn't, and now, especially, she was playing the commander role to the limit.

She'd been in charge of Lassen's European interests, involved mostly with smuggling, and now that Lassen—and their other partners—were dead, they were the only ones left to run the show.

"The plan is to lure Dane out here to rescue his girl-friend. Then we'll deal with them both."

"Where is Dane right now that we can't take care of him?"

"He's in a hospital bed, under guard at CIA headquarters. We don't have a chance at him there."

"How badly is he injured?"

"Not terribly, but it will be a few days before he's on his feet. Plenty of time to get ourselves situated. Where's the helicopter?"

"Camouflaged at our landing site about five minutes away. Pilot on standby."

"This is the climax of a battle I should have finished years ago, Helden."

"I'm not interested in your history. I have calls to make."

She started to leave the room.

"Stop."

She pivoted sharply.

"Once I call Dane, we need to split the men. I want some inside and some outside ready to counter-attack whatever raiding party Mr. Dane brings with him."

"You talk like he's some sort of superman."

"He'll bring friends, trust me."

"Do I get to play with the woman while we're waiting?"

"Do your worst, my dear."

She left the room, her shoes thunking on the wooden floor.

Royce took a breath and looked around. Every room in the place was bare, though this one had been set up as a sitting room with a bookcase. He didn't intend to be here long. Just long enough.

He looked in the direction Helden had gone. Calls to make, indeed. They had to make sure the other lieutenants in the organization didn't get ideas about bumping either of them off and taking over. He figured Helden was planning to shoot him at some point. She hadn't already done so because they had to deal with Dane. Once he was gone, all bets were off—meaning Royce had to get her first. Running a criminal enterprise was no different than running a spy ring. One had to be ruthless. Always.

They came for her that night.

Three troops grabbed Nina from the attic and dragged out her. She struggled on principle, but they were much stronger than her.

Presently they shoved her into a room on the ground floor. The room was empty except for a chair. They roughly shoved her onto the seat, then made quick work with ropes to secure her. When they departed, Helden Steuben stood in the doorway holding a barbed whip.

"Shouldn't you," Nina said, "be licking lard from a can?"

"You won't have such a smart mouth when I'm done with you."

"Usually Steve gets the torture scene," Nina said.

Steuben stepped forward. "Consider this," she said, "your contribution to female equality."

Nina flinched as the whip uncoiled. Helden Steuben moved her right arm in a flash, the barbed tip smacking into the center of Nina's chest, tearing through the fabric of her shirt. Nina screamed.

Helden Steuben ripped the shirt from Nina's body, using her left hand to feel the smoothness of the exposed skin, tracing fingers along her flat belly.

"How nice."

"I look like this," Nina said, "because I don't eat a month's worth of food for breakfast."

"Are you fat-shaming me?"

Helden Steuben stepped back and the whip cracked again, against bare skin this time. Nina bit back her yell as pain filled her body. She rocked back in the chair, trying to topple it backward, but the legs held firm. It must have been bolted. This room was the big woman's little torture chamber.

She slumped forward, gasping for breath.

"You can scream all you like," Steuben said. "The men like hearing the sound."

"You too?"

"It's soothing."

Nina didn't have enough saliva to spit as well as she would have liked, but she worked up enough, and spat at Steuben's feet.

"Keep fighting, dear," the big woman said. "Your night is only beginning."

The whip cracked again, and again, the barbed tip ripping at her chest, then her right cheek.

Her pulse raced and she stared blankly at the floor. There was no way out of this. She had to endure.

Dane stood by the window looking out on the courtyard below, with its greenery and benches and concrete, and thought it might be nice to open the window and let in some of the fresh air. But the pane was sealed tight.

He was on his feet for the first time in several days without feeling woozy or needing to grab on to the wall or bed rail. His biggest complaint was the draft from the air conditioner running up his backside, thanks to the opening in the hospital gown. Why hadn't there been some sort of patient revolution demanding something (a) better and (b) a little more dignified? If his condition forced an extended stay, he might try to organize the patients for just such an effort.

Lukavina had brought his cell phone, and it rested on the nightstand beside the bed, scuffed and cracked but still working. It had remained silent since Lukavina placed it there. What was Royce waiting for? Surely he had the number. If not, he could get it. Where was Nina? What was he doing to her?

Footsteps scraped the tiled floor behind him. Dane turned. Lukavina stood in the doorway with a surprised expression.

"You haven't fallen over?" the CIA man said.

"Still a little wonky but I think I can manage. Can we open this window at all?"

"That would take an order from Congress and require new windows," Lukavina said, coming up beside Dane to take in the view. "This is a government building, remember?"

Dane let out a laugh.

"Any noise from the cell?"

"Nothing," Dane said. "I'm beginning to think we'll have to do this the hard way."

"Shake cages?"

"Somebody always knows something. Lassen didn't exist in a vacuum."

And then the phone rang.

Dane moved quickly to pick it up from the nightstand and pressed the Talk button.

"Go."

"So you've been expecting me," Royce said.

"Terms. Now."

"No terms. A location. I want to see you in the Alps." Royce provided the location of his hideout, and Dane repeated it to Lukavina, who wrote it down in a pocket notebook.

"Three days or your woman dies."

Dane laughed. "You need to do better than that. There's a blonde in Barbados I've had my eye on for a while."

"Two days."

"You know I'm bringing the entire CIA with me, right?"

"I'd expect nothing less."

Royce ended the call. Dane put the phone down.

Lukavina said, "The entire CIA?"

"We need Royce alive if we're going to truly clear my father's name. I need whatever you can spare."

"Your father is already clear, Steve. Between the Gallagher file and everything we've collected from your little scorched-earth run, we know the story. Richard Dane is considered a victim of Royce's scheme. We don't need to take him alive if you don't want to."

"It's important that I bring him back. I can't explain why right now."

"I understand. You know we'll just throw him in a hole for the rest of his life, right? There's not going to be any public hearing on this."

"That's fine. Where are my clothes?"

"Are you sure you're ready?"

Dane started removing the hospital robe. "Get my clothes and throw in some painkillers just in case."

Chapter Forty-Four

Dane swallowed two tablets and stifled a groan as he tightened the top of his canteen.

"You need to be careful," Lukavina said.

They sat side by side against the fuselage of an agency jet, somewhere over the Atlantic Ocean heading for Switzerland. The strike team filled the rest of the cabin, their low voices and equipment checks background noise for Dane's throbbing head and sore body.

"Yeah," Dane said.

It felt good to see Lukavina kitted out for combat once again. Just like the old days. They were all dressed in black with equipment bags at their feet. Dane had asked for a pair of Micro Uzi machine pistols because of their compact size and firepower; in his condition, he thought they'd be easier to handle than the full-size M-4 carbine the rest of the team carried.

And at least the plane wasn't as uncomfortable and noisy as the C-130 Hercules transports of Dane's Marine past. This time there was padding on the bench seating, an insulated cabin to keep out the noise, and Wi-Fi. What they had done during long flights before Wi-Fi, Dane couldn't remember. He didn't want to remember. Wi-Fi was wonderful. When he died, he wanted to be buried near a hotspot just in case he could read The Conservative Treehouse every day in heaven.

Lukavina's left hand kept a tablet computer resting on his knee from hitting the floor. When the device beeped, he opened the front flap and tapped the screen. A note followed by a satellite photo appeared on the screen.

"We got the recon pics," Lukavina said.

The pictures showed Dane an overhead view of the Royce building and the surrounding countryside.

"What's that just due south?" Dane said.

Lukavina moved his fingers across the street to zoom in on the spot. "Looks like a badly camouflaged chopper."

Lukavina tapped the screen again, and the picture changed. The photographed area darkened but outlines of bodies filled the spaces.

"Infrared. It won't give us an exact count, but we'll at least have an idea of how many bodies we face."

"Some in the building and some in the hills there."

"He's trying to set up a crossfire. He knows we'll have this. What is he trying to do?"

"Final showdown. It's all or nothing."

"Even if you don't survive, we'll never stop looking for him. He has to know that."

"He does. He might have a plan for that. He doesn't have a plan for me," Dane said. He frowned and pointed at the building. "Zoom in on the hideout."

Lukavina made the picture larger. The outline of a body, stretched out and lying flat, occupied the upper area of the building. The body wasn't moving.

"Nina? In the attic?" Lukavina said.

"It's her."

"How do you know for sure?"

"You can't mistake the outline of her rear end."

Lukavina turned off the tablet. "Once we get on the ground and switch to the choppers, I have an idea for you," Lukavina said.

The pain didn't fade. Her whole body throbbed and the cuts on her chest and face remained tender.

The pain kept her alive.

Nina decided her left arm made a better pillow than her right, which had taken a few strikes from the barbed whip. Steuben had at least let her put on another shirt, the front of which was stained red.

She no longer had any sense of how long she'd been in the attic. Probably only two days, based on the cycle of the sun and the two-meals-per schedule they had her on. They never supplied proper utensils with her food, and she had to eat with her hands. Royce's crew weren't dummies. It hurt to sit up, so she remained on her side when eating.

She lay near the vent, the louvers opened as far as she could get them, on her side, resting her head on the fleshy upper part of her right arm. Staring out into the distance was becoming her only distraction; it wasn't much of one, because her thoughts kept intruding. It wasn't often she found herself caged without any means of escape. If there was a way out of here, she hadn't discovered it yet. But she kept scanning the horizon as if she was waiting for something. And she was. Steve had to be close.

The sky slowly turned dark after a bright pink sunset, and presently Nina dozed off, awakening with a start, still in the same place. She heard voices through the floor, muffled conversations she couldn't keep track of, but what sounded like the usual barracks bull roar. The scent of hot beef drifted through. Her stomach grumbled. What she needed more than anything was a rare steak and a beer.

A flash of light winked in the distance, followed by a low rumble and a puff of smoke over the hills. Nina pushed up and put her face close to the louvers. Then the ground came alive with a swarm of black-clad figures with automatic weapons, and the first blasts of gunfire split the night. The strike force spread out in a line, dropping as she heard louder gunfire emanate from the rooms below. The floor of the attic shook from the concussions and men screamed. Nina pulled back a little. No sense in her getting her face blown off by a stray round.

A helicopter roared overhead, a string of fire from a door-mounted machine gun chopping through the lower level of the building. The chopper flew over the top of the building, and then the roof shook from the shock wave of the rotor blades. Nina moved back to the center of the floor, staying flat. Were other troops going to rappel down?

Then she heard a voice over a loudspeaker: "Nina, honey, move to the west side of the roof!"

Dane's voice!

Her feet snagged on the carpet as she sprang for the far wall, facing the corner on her knees, bent over, hands clasped behind her neck.

Two loud blasts shook the roof some more. Air rushed in, bits of roof and shingle flying around, smacking into the walls. Nina turned. A big hole had been blasted in the roof and a rope dropped through, Steve Dane shimmying down, head to toe in black with a 12-gauge shotgun strapped across his back. He landed on the floor and tugged on the rope. It reversed through the hole and the rotor noise faded, the chopper pulling away. The machine gun fired again.

Nina rushed into Dane's arms, his heavy gear digging into her skin. She cried out. Dane pushed her away and he saw the splotches of red on her shirt.

"I'm fine," she said. "They said you were hurt!"

"I had a rough couple of days, but I'll live."

He pushed her away and handed her one of his Micro Uzi machine pistols.

"Can you fight?"

Pain etched Nina's face, but she nodded. "Watch me. I got a fat bitch to kill."

"How do we get out of here?" he said.

"That trapdoor," she said, pointing at the floor, "but it's bolted shut on the other side."

Dane whipped out the shotgun from the sheath on his back and shoved two rounds into the magazine tube. Nina covered her ears as he fired once, twice into the frame of the trapdoor, the panel dropping in several pieces to the hallway below.

Gunfire continued to hammer through the building and outside.

"You first," Dane said.

Nina sat down at the edge of the hole and dropped, landing in a crouch, staying low as she brought up the Micro Uzi and calling to Dane.

He dropped through next, dangling a second. And as his feet hit the carpet, Perry Royce came around the corner with a pistol flashing fire.

Chapter Forty-Five

Bullets cut the air between Nina and the dangling Dane. He dropped, landed and fell forward as more fire came from the barrel of Royce's gun. Nina fired back, tearing a chunk of plaster out of the wall where Royce hid, the debris pelting him in the face. He screamed, staggered into the open, his bum leg failing. He fell hard onto the carpet. Nina fired again as he fell, tearing up more wall behind him. Royce raised his gun as Dane lifted both his head and the Micro Uzi. Dane fired first, the flash of flame from the machine pistol creating a strobe effect in the hall. The salvo ripped into Royce's hip and lower leg, the man wailing. Dane gained his feet and ran to him, Nina watching with an open mouth. Dane didn't appear wounded or hurt at all. Dane reached the fallen man, first kicking the pistol out of Royce's hand and then kicking him again, this time in the head to knock him unconscious. Royce's wounds continued spilling blood into the carpet.

Nina remained on the floor, watching Dane. He pulled what looked like handcuffs from a pouch on his belt. She ran over to him. "Are you hit?"

"No," he said, rolling Royce onto his stomach to snap the cuffs on both wrists. "Afraid my legs are a little shaky. They done gave out on me."

"When we get home—" she started to say.

"Yeah," Dane said, rising. "When indeed." He pulled a radio from another pouch. "Royce is secured."

"We're moving in," said another voice, one Nina recognized as Lukavina's.

"Steve!"

Nina shoved Dane to the floor, bringing her Uzi up as Helden Steuben charged up the stairs with her own pistol.

Nina fired a burst. The salvo of rounds struck the big woman in the belly and stitched a line of holes to her neck, splashing her guts on the walls, the big woman's body falling to the bottom of the stairs where she landed in a heap.

"Promises made," Nina said, "promises kept."

She helped Dane to his feet.

"Good shooting, babe."

Nina's eyes didn't leave the body on the floor below.

Dane gave her a shove and they dragged Royce away from the staircase and back toward the hole leading to the attic. The firefight below intensified for a moment, several explosions shaking the walls, Dane and Nina standing ready with their weapons before them. But when the first two fighters ascended the steps and identified themselves, they lowered the guns and relaxed. The good guys had won. Now all that was left was the cleanup.

Dane and the CIA operatives carried Royce's body down the stairs and through the mass of strike force personnel and dead bodies.

Dane and Lukavina loaded Royce onto a stretcher and a medic started patching him up, plugging an IV drip into his left arm, and then they loaded him aboard the chopper. The rotor wash stirred up a fierce wind that whipped Nina's hair to and fro and the grass, too. She kept her head down as she followed Dane, Lukavina and Royce into the chopper's cabin, where the medic set Royce's stretcher in a corner.

Two more choppers came around a hillside as the first one lifted off.

Dane pulled Nina close and hugged her tightly.

"It's over," she said.

"A lot of things are over," he said. She felt his body deflate as he let out a sigh.

"How bad?" he asked her, gingerly feeling through her bloody shirt.

"I'm okay," she said. "Nothing that won't heal."

Dane didn't want to admit that he heard doubt in her voice.

When Royce opened his eyes, he found Dane sitting beside the stretcher, staring at him. The cabin was dark except for blue work lights, and they cast an odd glow over everything. Dane couldn't see Royce's face as clearly as he might have liked, but he could see it.

Royce tried to move his arms, but they were strapped to the stretcher. He lifted his head to look at his bandages, the IV drip. His head fell back, and he sucked a lungful of air. He moved his lips, croaking out words as he made eye contact with Dane. "Where am I?"

"Chopper," Dane said. "We're taking you back to the US."

"A trial?"

Dane shook his head. He didn't fight his smile. "Into a hole."

"Why didn't you kill me?"

The smile dropped from Dane's face.

"Tell me. You had every reason to kill me."

"Maybe I found a reason not to."

"I don't understand."

"I know."

Royce closed his eyes and remained quiet.

Dane scooted over to where Nina and Lukavina sat against the bulkhead. He put an arm around Nina and pulled her close. Lukavina said it wouldn't be much farther to the airport where the jet waited. Then they'd head straight for home.

Home. Dane liked the sound of that word.

Chapter Forty-Six

The CIA medical center hidden in the mountains of Virginia used for the treatment of field officers had all the amenities, and Nina, fresh from a shower, stood in front of the bathroom mirror looking at her naked body.

The marks from the barbed whip had been cleaned and treated, and the doctor didn't think the wounds would leave scars, but Nina had her doubts.

Her wounds inside were now on the outside. She couldn't deny them anymore or make them go away. All of her attempts to do so had failed.

She traced the lines of each wound, thinking about Wilmington, thinking about what happened in Moscow, replaying the words of the leader of the Trust, who called himself Number One, in her mind:

"We know what happened in Moscow, Ms. Talikova. You might say the two of you are on a collision course with what made you."

She sighed and dropped her arms to her side. Dane had settled his debts. Now it was time to settle her own.

The night's chill sent a shiver up Dane's spine.

He stood before John F. Kennedy's grave at Arlington, the eternal flame flicking in the semi-darkness. There was enough lighting around the memorial to give the area a soft glow. Dane turned as headlamps flashed behind him, stretching his shadow across the concrete. The black presidential limousine completed the turn in the circular driveway in front of the memorial and stopped. Dane approached the car, opened the back door and climbed inside.

The back cabin featured bench seats that faced each other, with space in the middle taken up by a small table on Dane's left. The man on the seat across from him sat with crossed legs and his hands in his lap, his blue suit still perfectly pressed.

"Good evening, Mr. President," Dane said.

"I see the candles worked," said Peter Cross.

"Did you light two?"

"Try three or four."

Dane chuckled. It felt good to laugh. The barriers he'd placed around himself were finally falling. Worse, he hadn't known they had been there or how they'd held him back. Shame had brought the barriers; shame about his father, because what if Dane had been wrong? Shame about running away instead of staying to fight. Maybe Cross had been right. All of his years on the run had brought him to this point; he was ready to finally grow up.

The limousine started moving, slowly, through the winding path around the cemetery. They'd decided it was the best place for their meeting. Quiet. Out of the way.

"You finally have a sense of peace about you, Steve."

"I feel it, sir."

Cross nodded. "I promise Perry Royce will never see

the sun again," the president said.

"I figured as much."

"Why didn't you kill him?"

"I met a man in San Remo," Dane said, "who would have done anything possible to kill me. I don't want to become that man."

Cross nodded again. "Probably for the best."

"It's time for the next chapter," Dane said. "Whatever that may be. A clean slate."

"It might be nice to have somebody you can call on when things really get bad."

"I like that idea very much. Of course, it won't be you on the phone."

President Cross laughed. "There has to be something I can do for you and Nina."

"She'd probably be happy with a case of booze, but I have a different favor to ask."

"Anything."

"I'd like to move my father's body here, to Arlington."

"Done."

Dane started to say something but paused, watching the man before him.

"You don't need to say anything more, son."

"Thank you, sir. I do need to say that. Thank you for everything."

"I hope you understand what I had to do."

"I do now," Dane said.

The limousine completed its circle and stopped once again at the eternal flame. Dane reached for the door handle.

"Until next time," he said, pushing the door open. Cool air flowed into the vehicle.

The president nodded and Dane exited the car, pushing the door closed. He watched the limo until it turned a corner and left the cemetery property. Putting hands in pockets, Dane turned and started to walk. Nowhere in particular, just forward, along the path taking him through the burial ground, where he could commune with the ghosts of battles past.

A Look At: Mine To Avenge: A Steve Dane Thriller

A desperate SOS from an old friend sends Steve Dane to the rescue only to find that he's too late.

Tom Wexler is dead and the stolen Iraqi antiquities he was trying to recover are gone again. With Nina Talikova by his side, Dane is determined to find out who killed his friend and restore a nation's history. But the game board is not in his favor, and when checkmate comes Dane discovers his enemies were once allies who know every move he'll make. In a winner-take-all contest against the toughest odds Dane and Nina have ever faced, they go on the offensive, not knowing if it will be good enough to save the treasures, or even their own lives.

An international thrill ride with two of the most dynamic characters in adventure fiction.

AVAILABLE August 2021

About the Author

A twenty-five year veteran of radio and television broadcasting, Brian Drake has spent his career in San Francisco where he's filled writing, producing, and reporting duties with stations such as KPIX-TV, KCBS, KQED, among many others. Currently carrying out sports and traffic reporting duties for Bloomberg 960, Brian Drake spends time between reports and carefully guarded morning and evening hours cranking out action/adventure tales. He lives in California with his wife and two cats, and when he's not writing he is usually blasting along the back roads in his Corvette with his wife telling him not to drive so fast, but the engine is so loud he usually can't hear her.